About the author

David Fuller is an FA-qualified
currently coaches a youth footba... ....ight.
He has worked as a journalist for more than a decade,
during which time he has written for numerous
publications on a variety of different subjects. David
lives in Newhaven, East Sussex with his wife, two
sons and cat Merry.

Other books by David Fuller

Alfie Jones and a change of fortune
Alfie Jones and a test of character
Alfie Jones and the missing link

To Amelia

RDF Publishing
3 Courtlands Mews, Church Hill, Newhaven,
East Sussex,
BN9 9LU

Alfie Jones and an uncertain future
A RDF Publishing book

First published in Great Britain by RDF Publishing in 2014
Printed and bound in the UK by Berforts Information Press,
King's Lynn.

1
Text copyright © David Fuller
Images courtesy of Rob Smyth
(www.robsmythart.com)

David Fuller asserts the moral right to
be identified as the author of this work

ISBN 978-0-9570339-3-1

For more exclusive Alfie Jones content, visit:
www.alfie-jones.co.uk

ALFIE JONES AND AN UNCERTAIN FUTURE

DAVID FULLER

**Illustrated by
Rob Smyth**

www.alfie-jones.co.uk

Chapter one

As he stared wide-eyed at the screen of his parents' computer, Alfie Jones simply couldn't believe what he was reading. There must have been some mistake. That was surely the only logical explanation.

There was just no way, none whatsoever, that Lakeland Spurs could really have beaten Ashgate Athletic 4-2.

Instinctively, Alfie clicked on the website's refresh button, certain that when the page reloaded the mistake would be rectified and Ashgate would have been shown to have won the match comfortably.

Much to his dismay, though, when the page reappeared nothing had changed.

The young boy rubbed vigorously at his big blue eyes, as if by doing so he would somehow be able to alter the score displayed on the screen in front of him.

A quick glance at the updated league table only served to further confirm Alfie's growing fear. The result was no mistake. It had really happened.

Alfie couldn't even begin to imagine how Lakeland Spurs had managed to beat Ashgate Athletic. Ashgate hadn't previously lost a league match all season, while Lakeland had started the day bottom of the table and had been thrashed 7-1 by the same team just three weeks earlier.

Well... they weren't bottom any more.

With only three games of the season remaining it was Alfie's very own Kingsway Colts under 11s who occupied the unwanted position of last place in Division 2 of the Middleton District Youth League.

Slumping back in his chair, Alfie's mind wandered back to Kingsway's own match against Southfield United earlier that day; more specifically to the chance he'd had to win the game just before the final whistle blew.

In fairness, it was by no means a simple

chance. He'd had to strike the ball first time from just outside the area, but while he'd managed to get his shot on target, he had been unable to generate enough power to seriously trouble the opposition goalkeeper.

The match had finished 2-2 and while at the time the Colts' players had felt that a draw was a decent result, looking at the league table now, Alfie couldn't help but feel that it wasn't quite good enough.

He looked at the league table again. Bottom! He could hardly believe it.

Only a few months earlier it would have been almost unthinkable to contemplate Kingsway's first season of competitive football being such a struggle.

They had started the season brilliantly; winning their first two league games and drawing with Ashgate in the third.

The team had seemingly made the jump up from 7-a-side football to 9-a-side with the minimum of difficulty, and Scott Foreman – the father of the Colts' best defender, Danny – had proved to be a popular replacement for the team's former coach Jimmy Grimshaw, who had left to take the Head Coach role at professional team Kingsway United's Elite Centre.

While Alfie had initially been extremely sad to see Jimmy leave the Colts, his despondency had soon turned to pleasure when he was invited to train at the Elite Centre – along with Colts' teammates Billy Morris, Hayden Whitlock and Liam Walker.

Alfie and Liam still attended the Elite Centre every Wednesday evening, but it hadn't taken long for Billy and Hayden to be promoted to United's under 11s Academy; a commitment that meant they were no longer allowed to play for the Kingsway Colts.

Unsurprisingly, the Colts' downturn in form had coincided directly with the loss of their two star players. Since Billy and Hayden's final game – the draw against Ashgate – the Colts had recorded just one win and two draws from their next 12 matches.

Alfie's hand hovered over the mouse button as he weighed up whether it would be worthwhile refreshing the page one more time, just in case... In the end, though, he decided that it would only prove to be a waste of time. Lakeland had beaten Ashgate, the Colts were bottom of the league, and that was that.

Usually, Alfie spent at least half-an-hour

on the Middleton District Youth League's website every Sunday evening. Without fail he'd check out how his school friends who played for other teams had got on, look up fixtures for the weeks ahead and even try to work out a set of results which would give the Colts the best chance of finishing as high up the table as possible.

His parents often joked – well, half joked – that if he spent only a fraction of the time studying his school work as he put into studiously scouring league tables and fixtures, then he'd have nothing to worry about from the upcoming end-of-Year 6 exams that he was soon due to sit.

However, he felt so deflated by the fact that the Colts had slipped to tenth – tenth sounded better than either 'bottom' or 'last', Alfie reasoned – that he had no desire to spend any longer on the website than necessary this evening.

He had barely turned off the computer when he heard his Mum calling him from the kitchen.

"Alfie, sweetie, the takeaway is here."

Usually the Jones family only had takeaways on Fridays, but Alfie had been staying at Billy's house on Friday night, while his younger sister Megan had been at a friend's slumber party, so

Mr and Mrs Jones had agreed, somewhat reluctantly, to a Sunday night takeaway instead.

It was Megan's turn to choose the type of takeaway they were having, and while Alfie had tried his hardest to persuade his sibling to go for pizza – his absolute favourite – he wasn't at all surprised to discover that she'd plumped for Chinese food. She always chose Chinese.

While Alfie didn't totally hate Chinese food, the truth was that he didn't overly care for it that much either. In fact, if it were up to him, he would be perfectly happy for his meals from the local Chinese restaurant to consist purely of prawn crackers. Now they were tasty!

However, his Mum and Dad always told him that he wasn't allowed any until he'd finished a good portion of his main meal first.

Determined to get to the prawn crackers before his sister, and therefore ensure that he got a bigger portion than Megan, Alfie set about devouring his sweet and sour chicken and egg fried rice as fast as he possibly could. No sooner had he shovelled the last mouthful of chicken and rice into his mouth – even though he still hadn't finished fully chewing his previous mouthful – did he dip his hand into the bag that the food had arrived in and yank out the prawn crackers.

"Steady on, Alf," Mr Jones warned, as, in his haste to get at the crackers, Alfie sent the entire contents of the bag flying across the dining room table.

"Whoopth. Thorry," Alfie spluttered, through a mouthful of food.

"Hey, what's this?" Megan asked, holding up something in a small red wrapper.

"It looks like a fortune cookie, Meggy," Mr Jones answered. "It's a biscuit that you split open, and inside there's a piece of paper which has something that's going to happen to you in the future written on it."

"Oh," Megan mused, taking a moment to think about what her Dad had just said. "I don't think I like the idea of that. What happens if it tells you something bad? I'm not sure I'd want to know if something bad was going to happen to me."

"Humph," Alfie snorted. "What a load of rubbish. Only a baby would believe something written on a piece of paper." There was only one person that Alfie believed when it came to predicting the future and that was Madam Zola – an elderly fortune teller that he had first met at a fun-fair more than two years earlier.

On that occasion, Madam Zola had told Alfie that he was going to be a professional footballer when he was older. Although he wanted to be a footballer more than anything, that wasn't the sole reason he'd ended up believing what the fortune teller had told him. She knew things about him that no one else could possibly know, and since their initial meeting she had helped him out on more than one occasion.

It had been a long time since Alfie had last seen or heard from Madam Zola, but he knew he'd see her again... one day... when he needed her.

So lost in thought had Alfie been, reminiscing about Madam Zola, that not only had he taken a few seconds' break from ramming prawn crackers into his already crammed mouth, but he'd also failed to realise that Megan had tossed the fortune cookie in his direction... until it hit him square on the forehead, that is.

"Owww! What did you do that for?" he whined.

"If you think it's so babyish, you open

it," Megan dared him.

Alfie rolled his eyes and then tore at the red packaging. Inside, just as his Dad had explained, was a small biscuit. Alfie snapped it in half and, sure enough, a piece of paper fluttered onto the table in front of him.

He picked it up, read it to himself, shrugged his shoulders, and then put it back on the table.

Megan glared at him. "What does it say? Tell me. NOW!"

Alfie sighed. "It just says that 'things will get worse before they get better.' It's a load of rubbish, though, like I told you. The Kingsway Colts are already bottom of the league. How can things possibly get any worse?"

"Maybe, just maybe, it's not about football, sweetie," stated Mrs Jones.

"Don't be so silly Mum," Alfie scoffed. "Everything is about football."

With that, he returned to stuffing prawn crackers into his mouth, quickly forgetting about the fortune cookie and what was written on the piece of paper.

It would only be much, much later, that Alfie would wish he had paid a bit more attention to that particular piece of paper.

Chapter two

Billy Morris could always tell how the Kingsway Colts had fared over the weekend just by noting the expression on Alfie's face as he entered the school playground on Monday morning.

In recent weeks he'd got used to seeing his best friend looking a tad dejected as he strolled into the school grounds, but nothing could have prepared him for how downcast Alfie looked this morning.

"Hi-ya, Alf," Billy called out as his buddy mooched miserably towards him.

Alfie nodded his head slightly by way of a greeting, but didn't say a word.

"I take it the Colts' lost again, then?" Billy asked, in what he hoped was a sympathetic manner.

To his surprise, though, Alfie shook his head. "Nope. We drew 2-2 with Southfield United."

"But Southfield are quite high up in the league, aren't they?"

"Fourth," Alfie agreed.

"Surely that's a good result, then? Why do you look so sad?" Suddenly a flash of panic worked its way through Billy's mind. Maybe football had nothing to do with why Alfie appeared to be so upset. Maybe it was something far more serious. "Is everything, okay, Alf?"

"Lakeland beat Ashgate," Alfie exclaimed. The shock of the result was still clearly audible in his voice. "We're bottom of the league!"

In truth, Billy should have known his best friend well enough to have ever doubted that the reason behind his irritation would be anything other than football-related. As much as he clearly loved the sport, nothing got Alfie quite so agitated as football.

"Sorry to hear that, Alf." He genuinely was, too. Although Billy was no longer allowed to play for the Colts due to his commitments with the Kingsway United Academy, he still wanted them to do well. They were the first team he'd ever played for and he was still good friends with all of the Colts' players.

"Never mind, I'm sure we'll win again soon," Alfie answered, although it was clear from the way he spoke that he didn't really believe a word of what he was saying. "How did you get on?" Alfie asked his pal, absent-mindedly.

"Err, we did okay," Billy replied vaguely. "Hayden played really well. I was only sub."

The truth was that Kingsway United's under 11s Academy team had beaten Premier League Westpool Athletic's Academy 5-2; Hayden had scored a hat-trick and Billy had himself set up two goals when he'd come on in the second half. Yet Alfie seemed so upset about the way things were going for the Kingsway Colts at present that Billy didn't want to make him feel even worse by bragging about how well he was doing.

Not that Alfie was really listening to what Billy was saying anyway. He was too busy staring across the playground at where Hayden and a few Colts' players were kicking a ball about to be fully concentrating on Billy's answer.

Liam Walker, Chloe Reed and Pranav Jamal were all laughing hysterically as they tried their best to get the ball off Hayden. The Academy player was dribbling past the other children as effortlessly as most people dribble around traffic cones. In the end, the only way they could relieve the ball from Hayden's possession was by Pranav and Liam wrestling him to the ground and then sitting on him while Chloe retrieved the ball.

"It's almost as if they don't even care that we're bottom of the league," Alfie sighed miserably, just loud enough for Billy to hear.

"I'm sure they do, Alf. They're just having, fun, that's all. Come on, let's go over and join them."

Alfie was in no mood to have fun, but before he could think of a polite way to refuse the offer, Liam and Pranav clambered off Hayden and sprinted away in another direction.

Hayden thought momentarily about giving chase, but then saw Billy and Alfie looking his way so he decided to jog over and join them instead.

"I guess I don't need to ask why you look so glum this morning, Alfie," stated Hayden once he'd joined his friends. "But it sounds like you guys played quite well

14

yesterday from what Pranav told me on the way to school."

"We're still bottom, though" moaned Alfie. "Not that anyone seems to care," he added, gesturing in the direction of some of the various Colts players who were scattered around the playground.

"To be honest, Pranav did seem quite gutted when he was telling me about it earlier," said Hayden. "I doubt Liam cares too much, though. He is probably going to be leaving the Colts next season, after all."

Alfie's mouth fell wide open while Billy turned to glare at Hayden, shaking his head slowly from side to side.

"WHAT!" Alfie yelled, a little louder than he'd intended.

"Nice one H," groaned Billy, clapping his hands together in a sarcastic manner.

"What?" asked Hayden, sounding more than a little confused. "Rickton Rovers have asked him to go and play for them next season and he wants to go because they're in the first division. I thought everyone knew that already? It was you that told me, Billy."

Alfie spun on his heels so that he was standing face-to-face with his best friend. "You knew?" he asked, struggling to contain the anger that was quickly boiling up inside him.

"Again... nice one H," said Billy, quickly glancing at Hayden, before looking once more at Alfie. "I only found out on Saturday, Alf," he explained. "Reuben told me at training." Reuben Ryan was a former Rickton Rovers player who currently played for the Academy alongside Billy and Hayden. "I was going to tell you this morning, but you seemed so down that I thought I'd wait a while. How was I to know that clever clogs here," he pointed at Hayden, "was going to open his big mouth?"

"Sorry, I thought if you knew then he'd know. It's not my fault, you hadn't told him yet," snapped Hayden, who thought it was more than a little unfair that he was being blamed for a genuine misunderstanding.

"But he's one of our best players," said Alfie despairingly, the anger in his voice quickly being replaced by a mixture of sorrow and frustration. "If he leaves then..."

Before Alfie could complete his sentence, though, Chloe came bounding towards them.

"Hi boys," the Colts' only female player

16

called to them as she skipped closer.

"I suppose you already know about Liam and Rickton Rovers," said Alfie, without so much as uttering a hello to one of his oldest and closest friends.

Chloe's cheeks immediately flushed bright red. "Yeah, I know" she admitted. "He told me on Friday. Err... look, Alfie, there's probably something else I should tell you..."

Alfie only had to see the expression on Chloe's face to be able to guess what was coming next. "Don't tell me you're thinking about leaving the Colts as well?"

Chloe nodded sheepishly. "I'm sorry, Alfie. I love playing for the Colts, really I do. It's just that... there's a girls' youth team starting up in Kingsway, and I think it would be better for me to go and play for them next season. I'd only have to move over to girl's football in a few years anyway. So why not go now?"

Even Alfie had to admit that this was a fair enough reason for leaving. Far better than Liam's, anyway, who as far as Alfie was concerned only wanted to leave to play for a better team, giving no consideration at all to his current teammates and, more importantly, friends.

"I don't believe this," Alfie moaned. "First Jimmy leaves, then Billy and Hayden, and now you and Liam. We won't have enough players for a team next season at this rate."

Suddenly a look of real horror passed over Alfie's face. For the second day running he found himself thinking back to his first ever meeting with Madam Zola. During that meeting the fortune teller had told him quite clearly that his destiny to become a professional footballer would only come true if he stayed playing for the Colts – something that hadn't appeared likely at the time.

But what happened if there was no longer a Kingsway Colts team for him to play for?

Alfie couldn't stop himself from thinking that his destiny to one day become a professional footballer could be under serious threat.

Chapter three

Being in Year 6 certainly had its
advantages.

Every single break time, providing
it wasn't raining, Alfie and his friends
would take over a sizable section of the
school playground, mark out a pitch using
their bags, jumpers or coats, and then
split into two teams and play football
until the teacher on duty rang the bell to
signal the end of break.

It was a privilege reserved only for the
oldest year group at Kingsway Junior
School.

If it happened to be raining, then Alfie
and co would simply attempt to get a
similar game going inside the classroom...
well, until one of the Year 6 teaching

assistants invariably put a stop to such proceedings, that is.

By 10:30 that morning, however, Alfie was feeling so miserable that, for the first time in seven months of being in Year 6, he just couldn't bring himself to join in with the break time kick-around.

Billy, Chloe, Hayden, Pranav and Liam had all taken turns to try and persuade Alfie to participate in the game, but he declined all their offers, refusing point blank to speak to Liam at all.

Ever since Billy had been selected for the Kingsway United Academy, Alfie had arguably spent more time with Liam than he had with any of his other friends. It was now Liam's Dad, instead of Billy's, who gave Alfie a lift to and from Colts' matches and training sessions each week, while he also took him to the Kingsway United Elite Centre on Wednesday evenings too.

Yet, in spite of the many hours the two boys had spent together on the back seat of Mr Walker's car, not once had Liam dropped even the slightest hint to Alfie regarding the possibility of him leaving the Kingsway Colts.

To make things even worse, everyone else already seemed to be aware of his intentions. It was this that had left Alfie seething with anger.

In truth, there was a part of Alfie that could totally understand Liam's frustrations. The fact was that he hadn't particularly enjoyed losing so many games this season either, and being bottom of the league table so close to the end of the season was a truly horrible feeling. But he also strongly believed that if the team just stuck together for another season then things would soon start to improve.

Back when Jimmy Grimshaw had been the Kingsway Colts' coach, he'd always gone to great lengths to explain to the children that playing football for enjoyment alongside your friends was far more important than winning every week; especially at a young age.

"Enjoy playing first and foremost," Alfie could clearly recall the elderly coach telling the team just before their first ever match three years earlier. "If you don't enjoy playing then you will never, ever improve! Don't put any pressure on yourselves and play without fear. Just get out on to the pitch, do your best, try different skills, and always encourage your teammates. Do all of these things and before you know it you'll soon start getting the results you deserve."

The Colts had ended up losing that first match 7-2, yet every single player walked off the pitch at the end of the game with the widest of smiles on their faces. When the Colts' played the same team again later on that season, they won 4-3.

As Alfie sat by himself on one of the benches located at the side of the playground, half watching Billy and Hayden run rings around most of the other Year 6 children who were taking part in the break time match, he couldn't stop his lips from curling upwards to form a small smile as he thought back to Jimmy's pre-match team-talks; most of which would inevitably end with the same two words – "enjoy it".

'Did he never listen to anything Jimmy told us about playing alongside friends?' Alfie wondered as he watched Liam receive an inch perfect pass from Hayden and then fire the ball between two tatty blue school jumpers which had been used to mark out a goal. Liam may not have been as good an all-round player as either Billy or Hayden, but he certainly knew how to score goals. He'd scored 21 of the Colts' 37 total goals so far this season, and had finished as the team's top scorer in each of the previous two seasons.

Alfie had only been watching his friends play for about a minute when he started to become aware of just how much he was missing being involved in the game. However, having been so dismissive towards his friends when they'd urged him to come and play only a few moments before, he thought he'd look a bit foolish if he was to go and get involved now. 'I'll just wait until lunch and play then,' he decided.

Yet, the more he watched his friends having fun, the more desperate he became to go and join in with their game.

Not wanting to swallow his pride and have to admit to his friends that he'd been wrong to say he didn't want to play, Alfie cast his eyes around the playground, searching for someone he knew who wasn't playing football. There were only ten minutes of break left; surely if he could find someone to talk to he could make it to the start of the next lesson without having to give in to temptation.

He spotted Megan and some of her Year 3 friends tucked away in the far corner of the playground playing hopscotch, but there was absolutely no way that Alfie was going to spend break time with his little sister – he saw quite enough of her at home!

Standing close to Megan's group, however, were a group of Year 5 boys, all of whom he knew pretty well. They appeared to be swapping football cards and although Alfie didn't have any cards with him to swap, he figured he could at least have a chat with them about football to pass the remainder of break time.

He was just about to start walking towards them when he suddenly noticed that he had not been the only Year 6 boy moping around at the side of the playground.

Seated on another bench just a couple rows along from him, seemingly staring into thin air, was the rather imposing figure of Jasper Johnson.

Jasper and Alfie had never got on with one another. Their rivalry stretched back to the time when Jasper had briefly played for the Kingsway Colts and his Dad, Keith, had been the team's temporary coach. It had been a miserable period for Alfie and he'd come extremely close to quitting the Colts.

In recent months, though, Jasper had

not seemed to be as confident and brash as he once was.

Ever since he'd been discarded by the Kingsway United Academy, thanks mainly to a discovery made by Alfie with the help of Jimmy Grimshaw, Jasper had kept himself to himself.

He didn't really seem to have any friends at the school. In class he sat on a single desk at the back of the room where nobody could bother him, and he never joined in the break time football match.

In fact, Billy had recently told Alfie that Jasper hadn't so much as kicked a football since his experience at the Academy had ended so sourly, and while Keith still coached North Malling Town Under 11s, Jasper never played for them.

As he continued to stare in Jasper's direction, Alfie couldn't help but feel a pang of sympathy for him. Sat by himself at the bench he just looked so lonely and forlorn.

Maybe now was the ideal time to put their silly rivalry behind them and to make friends.

For a second or two, Alfie stood rooted to the spot, torn between going to join the group of Year 5 boys and attempting to strike up a conversation with Jasper.

Against his better judgement he plumped for the latter option.

It was a decision he would instantly regret.

Chapter four

Alfie had walked no more than halfway to the bench when Jasper turned his head and glared directly at him. It was clear from the look on his face that he did not wish to be disturbed.

"What do you want?" Jasper asked, the disdain he felt for Alfie clear from his tone.

Alfie hesitated for a moment. It wasn't too late for him to change his mind. He could just walk straight past Jasper and head towards the main school building; pretend he needed to use the toilet or something.

'No,' he thought to himself. 'I decided to speak to Jasper and that's just what I'm going to do.'

He walked the rest of the way to the bench and then sat down next to the other boy, much to Jasper's obvious annoyance.

The size difference between the two boys was startling; it was almost impossible to believe that they were in the same school year. While Alfie was slightly smaller than average for an 11-year-old boy, Jasper was gigantic. His blue school jumper barely fitted him, even though he was wearing the largest size available, while Alfie was fairly sure that he was wearing a pair of Keith's trousers – and even those looked a tad snug around his waist

Yet while Alfie had once been intimidated by Jasper's sheer size, he wasn't anymore. "I was just wondering how you are? I haven't spoken to you for ages. Not since..." Alfie paused, trying to remember the last time he'd actually spoken to Jasper.

"Since you got me kicked out the Kingsway United Academy last year?" Jasper sneered.

Alfie felt his cheeks burn a little. He desperately hoped that he wasn't blushing. "Well... err... that's not exactly what happened. If you remember..."

"Save it," snapped Jasper, angrily. "I don't want to hear your excuses. Just go away and leave me alone."

At that point Alfie should have done just as he was being instructed. But he'd resolved in his mind to try and make peace with Jasper so that was exactly what he was going to attempt to do.

"Look, Jasper, I'm really sorry that things didn't work out for you at the Academy, and I'm also sorry if you think that was my fault. But don't let that disappointment put you off playing football totally. Why don't you come in and join our game at lunchtime? I'm sure the others won't mind."

Immediately the harsh look on Jasper's face began to soften. He started to smile – not a particularly pleasant smile, but a smile nonetheless – and then, much to Alfie's surprise, he started to laugh uncontrollably.

"What's so funny?" Alfie asked, pleased to have seemingly brightened Jasper's dour mood.

"Y... y... you...," gasped Jasper in between fits of hysterical giggling. "You're what's so funny." Jasper took a deep breath in a bid to regain his composure. "Let me get this straight. You think the

29

reason I choose not to join in your stupid break time games is because I'm too upset to play football anymore." He'd barely completed the sentence before he broke into another fit of giggles. He was laughing so much that tears were streaming down his cheeks.

"Well, isn't it?" Alfie enquired, a look of confusion etched on his face.

Jasper took another long, deep breath and waited for the giggles to subside. "Oh, you really are a muppet aren't you? The reason I don't join in your childish break time matches is that I'm just far too good for you lot. What would be the point? I was part of an Academy team not so long ago. Why would I want to lower myself to playing with a bunch of losers like you lot?"

Alfie was stunned to hear what the larger boy was saying. Jasper had only been selected for the Kingsway United Academy as part of a sneaky plan to significantly weaken the club's youth set-up. Both boys had been present when that truth had been revealed – how could Jasper still think that he was a better footballer than everyone else?

"But Jasper..." Alfie started, not quite sure how to phrase the next question he wanted to ask. "What about what happened at the Kingsway United Academy?"

"What about it," Jasper answered, gesturing dismissively. "United are a League One club. Small time. Who cares what they think. My Dad's promised me that he'll get me into a Premier League Academy... and he always keeps his promises."

Alfie shook his head sadly. When would Jasper learn that he just wasn't anywhere near as good a player as he believed he was? "So... Why don't you play for your Dad's team anymore then?"

Jasper sighed, as if the answer was too obvious for him to have to explain. "Because he doesn't want to risk me getting injured and then having to miss out on my Academy trial... when he sorts one out for me."

He started laughing again. "I really can't believe that you thought the reason I sit here by myself rather than join in your stupid games was because I'm too upset to play football. I'm a winner, muppet, unlike you. With my talent, it will only be a matter of time before I hit the big time. Still, it must be hard for you, still plugging away at the Elite

Centre while Billy and Hayden are at the Academy. Face facts Alfie, you're being left behind. You'll never be good enough to be a professional football player."

These words hurt Alfie more than he would ever let on. While he was naturally delighted that his two friends were doing so well, especially Billy, there was still a part of him that was slightly – actually, extremely – jealous of their success too; he yearned to be in the Academy alongside them.

Nevertheless, he remained totally confident that he would still one day become a professional footballer. Madam Zola had told him that it was his destiny to do so. She'd also told him that he had to stay with the Colts in order to make his destiny come true. Well, he couldn't stay with the Colts if he was picked for the Academy so maybe, he had reasoned to himself on more than one occasion, that was the reason why he hadn't been selected yet.

"From what I hear," Jasper continued, clearly starting to enjoy his tirade, "you won't even be a Kingsway Colts player for much longer. What, with Liam and Chloe leaving and you lot already being rubbish and bottom of the league, I can't see you having enough players to field a team next season."

Alfie couldn't believe what he was hearing. Even Jasper knew about Liam and Chloe's plans to leave the Colts. How was that possible when he'd only found out earlier that morning?

"Just because I don't sit near or speak to you lot, doesn't mean I don't hear things," said Jasper, as if he could read Alfie's mind. "Never mind, muppet, maybe you could try having a go at another sport next year. Netball ought to suit you."

With that Jasper stood up, ruffled Alfie's blond curly hair in a highly patronising manner, and strolled off in the direction of the school, laughing loudly as he went.

Alfie stayed seated on the bench for a few moments more, silently admonishing himself for ever thinking that trying to make friends with Jasper could possibly have been a good idea.

While he knew that most of what Jasper had said was as deluded as ever – especially with regards to Keith getting him a trial at a Premier League club – there was undeniably some truth in what his former teammate had said about the Kingsway Colts struggling to get a team together next season. It was the exact same thought he'd had earlier that morning.

With Hayden and Billy no longer allowed to play for them, and Liam and Chloe looking certain to leave at the end of the season, Alfie couldn't rid himself of the feeling that it would only be a matter of time before other players also decided to leave the Colts. 'Who knows,' thought Alfie, 'if Madam Zola hadn't told me that I have to stay with the Colts in order to become a professional footballer, then maybe I'd be thinking about leaving as well?'

Once again the words Madam Zola had spoken to him during their first meeting more than two years earlier came flooding back to him: "Stay with the Colts and one day you will become a professional footballer." He could remember the fortune teller uttering that sentence as clearly as if she'd only said it to him yesterday.

The more he thought back to that first meeting with Madam Zola, the more desperate Alfie became to see her once again.

He wanted – no, he needed – to ask her whether the warning she'd given him back then still mattered now. Did he definitely have to remain a Colts player in order to one day become a professional footballer?

He was only too aware, though, that Madam Zola would only present herself to him when she was good and ready.

He just hoped that would be sooner rather than later.

Chapter five

The atmosphere in the back of Mr Walker's car as he drove to the Kingsway United Elite Centre that Wednesday evening could not have been any tenser.

Ten minutes had passed since Liam's Dad had picked Alfie up from outside his house and the two boys were yet to say a single word to each other. They both just sat in complete silence, moodily staring out of the window located closest to their seat.

Liam had tried speaking to Alfie on numerous occasions at school over the past couple of days, but every time he'd attempted to strike up a conversation with his friend, Alfie had simply blanked him.

Earlier that day, Liam had started to ask Alfie if he needed a lift to the Elite Centre later. Before he could even finish asking his question, though, Alfie had strolled off in another direction.

"I can't be bothered with this anymore," Liam told Hayden, during the afternoon maths lesson. "If he doesn't want to speak to me, then I'm not going to speak to him either! Oh, can you do me a favour and ask him if he wants a lift to the Elite Centre tonight. Tell him that my Dad will pick him up at the normal time if he does."

And so it was that as Mr Walker drove through the early evening traffic, en-route to the 3G astroturf pitch where the Elite Centre held its training sessions, an uncomfortable silence filled the car.

At first Mr Walker had found the peace and quiet to be quite pleasant. He was usually forever telling the two boys to keep their noise down so that he could hear the radio. However, he'd soon started to find the lack of noise coming from the backseats a little unsettling.

"What is up with you two this evening?" he asked after a further five minutes of noiselessness. "You two normally don't stop jabbering from the moment you get in the car to the moment you get out. Tonight you haven't said so much as a word to one another. What's going on?"

"Nothing," grunted Liam.

"Nothing," grouched Alfie.

"If you say so," replied Mr Walker, sceptically.

After another few minutes of awkward silence had drifted by, Liam's Dad decided to have another go at getting a conversation started. "Looking forward to the match against Health Hill on Sunday, boys? I reckon you'll beat them if you play like you did against Southfield last week."

"Hopefully," agreed Liam.

"Huh, like you care," Alfie mumbled.

"What's that supposed to mean?" Liam retorted, angrily.

"Nothing," answered Alfie, sullenly.

"No, come on, out with it. Why wouldn't I care whether we win or not? Of course I care. I hate losing all the time."

Mr Walker was starting to wish that he'd kept his mouth shut and let the silence continue.

"Why would you care?" Alfie exploded, as the anger he'd kept bottled up for the past three days came spilling out. "You're not going to be a Colts player next season

38

anyway. Hayden told me all about your plans to join Rickton Rovers next season. I can't believe you're going to leave the Colts just because we're having one bad season!"

"Ha – I knew this was the reason why you've got the hump with me," exclaimed Liam. "And who says I'm leaving anyway? I haven't made up my mind yet. One of the Rickton players asked me to join them and I said 'maybe'. If you'd bothered to ask me about it rather than choosing to ignore me all week then you'd have known this already."

"You should have just told me that you were thinking about leaving in the first place," replied Alfie, his tone softening slightly. "We spend loads of time together now. It was horrible hearing about it from other people," he added.

"I haven't actually told anyone, well apart from Dad," said Liam, shrugging his shoulders. "The Rickton player told Reuben Ryan that he'd asked me to play for them, Reuben told Billy and he told Hayden. From there the news just spread really, really quickly."

"Oh," stuttered Alfie. He was starting to feel a little guilty about the way he'd been treating his friend over the past few days.

"For what it's worth..." began Mr Walker, who was clearly relieved the bickering that he'd inadvertently started seemed to have stopped. "... I think Liam should give it another season with the Colts. But, as I've already told him, if he does decide to leave then it's his decision. I just want him to play somewhere where he'll be happy."

"I honestly don't know what to do, Alfie," continued Liam. "I've always really enjoyed playing for the Colts, but it's just not been the same this season, what with Billy and Hayden no longer being able to play for us and Jimmy not involved anymore. I hate losing all the time as well and I really don't want to be playing in division 3 next season – that's the division that North Malling Town are in, and they're rubbish. Plus Rickton are one of the best teams in the area. They're near the top of the first division. Imagine how many goals I'd score if I was playing for them!"

Alfie nodded. There was little doubt that Rickton Rovers were one of the best teams that the Colts had ever played against and Liam would certainly get lots of goalscoring chances if he were to go and play for them. Nevertheless, he was desperate for Liam to give it another season with the Colts but, try as he might, he couldn't think of anything to say that might persuade Liam to stay.

"I'm going to ask Jimmy what he thinks I should do after tonight's session," added Liam, deliberately nodding his head. "He always gives good, fair advice."

Soon afterwards, Mr Walker pulled into a car parking space just outside the entrance to the 3G pitch. The two boys exited the car in a rather better mood than when they'd entered it. Alfie had apologised for the way he'd been behaving towards Liam since Monday morning, while in turn Liam promised Alfie that he would be the first to know once he'd made his decision about who to play for next season.

An hour and a half later, as Jimmy Grimshaw collected a few stray jumpers and jackets that some of the boys had left lying about on the side of the pitch, Liam and Alfie rushed over to him.

"Jimmy I need some advice," stated Liam.

"Okay Liam. Fire away."

"He's going to ask you about leaving the Colts," Alfie blurted out, unable to stop himself. "That would be a mistake,

41

though, wouldn't it? Tell him Jimmy. Tell him to stay with the Colts."

Jimmy frowned and looked carefully at Liam, who in turn was glaring at Alfie. "Is this true, Liam? Why ever would you want to leave the Colts?"

Slowly but surely, Liam explained his situation to the elderly coach, giving him the exact same details that he'd given Alfie in the car. Once he'd finished talking, Jimmy looked thoughtful for a few moments. It was clear to both boys that he was carefully weighing up what to say next.

"Let me tell you a quick story," he began eventually. "When I was a young boy, probably around your age, I played for a team that wasn't doing that well – we certainly lost more games than we won. There was another local team who tended to win most weeks and after a while a lot of our better players went and joined them. Well, as you can imagine, for the next couple of seasons we continued to struggle while the other team won loads and loads of games. Then, suddenly, one season things changed. Just like that," the old coach clicked his fingers.

"We started winning practically every week, while the other team started to struggle. They'd kept changing their team at the beginning of each season, you see, constantly looking for better players. The outcome was that they became a group of individuals rather than a team. We stuck together, started playing as a team and ended up being far more successful than them – even though our players arguably weren't as good. Football is a team sport, after all."

"So you agree with me then," declared Alfie triumphantly. "You think Liam should stay with the Colts."

Again Jimmy paused before answering. "Maybe. Youth football has changed a lot since I were a lad. It really depends on

what you're looking for, Liam. If you want
to play with your friends and improve
together, then you should definitely stay
with the Colts. If you want to try and
force your way into the Academy, like
Hayden and Billy already have, then you
need to be playing with the best players
possible. Division 2 is an okay standard,
but most professional teams, including
Kingsway United unfortunately, don't
tend to send scouts to many games
outside of the top two leagues in each
age group. That said, going to play for
Rickton doesn't necessarily mean you'll
definitely get picked for the Academy, and
you'll probably find that there will be a
lot more competition for places, so you
may end up playing fewer games than
you do at the moment."

It was clear from the look on Liam's face
that he was now even more confused than
he had been prior to speaking to Jimmy.
"I just don't know what to do," he sighed.

Alfie fought back the urge to yell 'stay
with the Colts' at the top of his voice.

Suddenly Jimmy clapped his hands
together excitedly. "I've got an idea," he
declared. "How does this sound? If the
Colts end up avoiding relegation from
division 2, then you stay with them.

If they get relegated then you move to Rickton."

Liam smiled. "That is a good idea," he said.

"But we're bottom of the table," moaned Alfie.

"Yes, but from what I recall you're only two points behind the team in eighth, and you're playing them on Sunday," explained Jimmy. He may not have been the Colts' coach anymore, but that didn't mean that he no longer kept a close eye on their progress. "If you win that, and Lakeland Spurs also lose, or even draw, you'll be out of the bottom two. You've still got every chance of staying up."

Liam's smile broadened and he started to nod his head. "Okay," he agreed. "That's fair. Thanks Jimmy."

Alfie could already feel the butterflies starting to form in the pit of his stomach. The last three games of the Kingsway Colts' season had just taken on some extra significance.

Chapter six

It may have seemed like a good idea at the time, but it didn't take long for Alfie to realise that he'd made a mistake.

During the Colts' training session on Saturday morning, he had spoken to a couple of Kingsway's better players about the agreement Liam had made with Jimmy on Wednesday evening.

He figured that when some of his teammates realised that the team's star striker would definitely stay with the Colts if they could avoid relegation, then they would be sure to put extra effort into getting the results they needed to make sure the team didn't finish in the bottom two positions.

Unfortunately the conversation that

he'd had with Des Grey and Luke Stanford hadn't gone quite how he'd imagined it would.

"That is a good idea," Des mused. "I hadn't really thought about what would happen if we finish bottom of the league but, now you mention it, I don't really want to play in division 3 either. If we get relegated I'll probably just join another team too."

"Well if Des goes to another team, so am I," added Luke. "He's my best friend!"

"B... b... but what about the Colts?" spluttered Alfie. "You can't just leave the Colts. We have to make sure we don't get relegated."

"Why?" asked Des. "There are plenty of other teams around here to play for. We could just join one of them instead."

"But you've been one of the Colts from the beginning, Des," Alfie continued, a note of pleading had by now entered his voice. "You have to stay. Won't you miss playing for the Colts?"

Des shrugged his shoulders. "Not really," he replied after a short pause. "Playing for the Colts isn't the same as it used to be, Alfie. Not without Jimmy, Billy or Hayden. Chloe's definitely leaving and, from what you've just told me, possibly Liam too. What's the point of staying? There are other teams Alfie, it's not like you have to stay with the Colts forever."

'I might have to actually,' Alfie had mumbled to himself, as Des and Luke ran off to join the rest of the team for their warm-up.

Later that day, Alfie was sat perched on the end of his bed, thinking through some of the options that would be available to him if the results of the Colts' final games didn't go the way he hoped.

It was now almost certain that unless the team avoided relegation there would no longer be a Kingsway Colts team for him to play for next season.

If the worst happened, and Liam, Des, Luke and, of course, Chloe, all ended up going to play for new teams, then it was plainly obvious that without finding new players the Colts wouldn't be able to continue. Alfie supposed he could always try and get new players to sign, but the truth was he couldn't really think of anyone he knew that would be interested.

He was only too aware that a more likely outcome was that once so many players left, Danny would probably also want to leave, which would mean his Dad would no longer want to coach the team.

'I suppose I could always just look for another team as well,' Alfie mused silently to himself. 'But does that mean my destiny won't come true? I really do need to speak to Madam Zola.'

As the week had gone on, Alfie had become increasingly frustrated by the fact that he'd still not heard from Madam Zola. She always seemed to turn up when he needed her. Well he needed the old fortune teller now more than ever! Where was she?

Alfie leaned across his bed and grabbed a notebook and pen from his bedside table. He was sure the pen had been a present from Madam Zola. It had been left on the windscreen of Billy's Dad's car while the Colts were playing in their first ever football tournament two summers ago, and on closer inspection Alfie had found that the initials 'MZ' were inscribed on it.

He began to write down a list of all the places he'd previously met the fortune teller; maybe if he revisited each one, then he might see her again.

However, he'd only got halfway through the list when his concentration was broken by Megan walking into his room.

As ever, she hadn't bothered to knock before entering.

"Wow! I didn't know you could write Alfie," laughed his little sister, as she tossed one of her magazines onto the bed beside him.

"Go away Megan. I'm not in the mood," warned Alfie, without looking up from his notepad.

"Well Mum told me to come and tell you that it's nearly dinner time, so you need to go and wash your hands."

Alfie let out an exasperated sigh. "In a minute, I'm busy. Now go away," he replied.

"But mum said now," continued Megan, steadfastly refusing to leave his room. "I'll just wait here until you're ready."

"Just get out of my room, Megan," Alfie ordered. His younger sister had an uncanny habit of getting under his skin in a way that no one else could. "And take your stupid mag with you," he added, picking up the magazine she'd thrown at him a few second earlier.

"Oh, that's for you to look at. I thought you'd be interested to read what's on that page. You can read, can't you?"

Alfie tutted loudly. "Of course I can read, but I've got no desire to read about

50

what pop star is going out with another pop star. It just doesn't interest me. Now take it and go away."

"Just read it," insisted Megan.

Alfie glanced at the page. "Mystic Jane Folies' guide to the future," he said aloud, before looking up at his sister. "Megan, this is a horoscopes page. Why would I be interested in reading a horoscopes page?"

"Just read yours," Megan urged. "Please, please, please, please..."

Although Alfie had no desire whatsoever to read his horoscope, he also knew that, unless he did, his sister would only continue to say please until she ran out of breath – which could take a week or more!

He quickly scanned the page for his star sign, Libra, and then began to read it out loud.

"Things haven't been going well for you recently. You desperately need someone to talk to, but there's never anyone around when you need them. Be prepared, as over the coming weeks things will get worse before they get better, but rest assured, they will get better soon."

"Isn't it amazing," yelped Megan

51

excitedly as soon as he'd finished reading.

Alfie couldn't have looked more confused if he tried. "What? It's just a load of old rubbish? These things never come true. They're just made up."

"Well that's where you're wrong," stated Megan, smugly. "My horoscope said that I'd come into some money this month and I've just found 50p in the hallway."

Alfie quickly checked his pockets. "Hey, that's my 50p," he whined. "It must have fallen out of my pocket earlier."

"Yeah well, finder's keepers. Anyway, back to the magazine, don't you see?"

"See what?" Alfie was now really starting to reach the end of his tether with the conversation.

"Your horoscope says exactly the same thing as that fortune cookie last week. 'Things will get worse before they get better.' Weird or what?"

"Amazing," said Alfie, in a tone designed to suggest that his sister's discovery was anything but. Secretly, though, he did think it was a bit odd.

"You know what this means, don't you? What was written in that fortune cookie must really mean something. I told you that you should believe what it said."

"It could also mean that Jane Folies, or

whatever her name is, gets her Chinese takeaways from the same place that we do. Now get out of my room."

With that Alfie threw the magazine as hard as he could in his sister's direction, aiming for her head. However, Megan had been expecting such a move and had already ducked out of the way.

Rather than hitting its intended target, the magazine instead fluttered harmlessly over Megan's head and flew into a shelf behind her, knocking a few items onto the floor.

"Oh, you knocked your little teddy bear off the shelf," said Megan in a mocking tone, as she scooped up the teddy that was decked out in a blue football kit. It was another one of the gifts that Madam Zola had given to Alfie and it now acted as his lucky mascot. "Does the baby need his bear back?" she asked, as if speaking to a toddler.

Much to Megan's annoyance, though, her attempt to further anger her older brother had failed. Alfie was no longer paying her any attention. He was too busy staring at the bear she was holding.

An idea was starting to form in his mind. It was a long shot, to be sure, but it was an idea nevertheless.

Chapter seven

The following morning Alfie woke even earlier than he usually did on the day of a game.

Although feeling nervous on the morning of a match wasn't a new experience for him – it was a weekly occurrence, in fact – Alfie honestly couldn't remember having ever felt quite as apprehensive ahead of a match as he did now.

Thoughts of how the game against Heath Hill United would go had been running through his mind all night; rendering sleep practically impossible.

Win the game, Alfie speculated, and the Colts had every chance of avoiding relegation. Surely, he reasoned – or, more accurately, hoped – the confidence that the team would gain from finally winning a match after such a long time would give the Colts' players the belief they needed to get the required results from their remaining two fixtures.

If they were to lose, however... well, he'd tried his best not to think about what would happen if they lost; albeit without much success.

Climbing out of bed, Alfie crept as quietly as he could down the hallway, not wanting to wake his parents, or even Megan, at such an early hour. Reaching his Dad's office, which was little more than a tiny box room located at the opposite end of the hallway from his bedroom, Alfie slipped silently through the door and switched on his parents' computer.

Once it had loaded, Alfie logged on to the Middleton District Youth League website and clicked on to the Under 11s Division 2 league table.

While he may not have been able to bring himself to study the table last Sunday evening, this morning he wanted a clear picture of what the Colts were facing from their remaining three fixtures.

Ignoring the top six places, Alfie cast his eyes down to the teams in seventh, eighth, ninth and, with considerable effort, tenth place. Seeing the Colts bottom of the table still saddened him immensely.

A quick analysis of the league table merely served to reiterate the importance of the day's game, and further multiplied the butterflies already floating around in his tummy.

	P	W	D	L	F	A	Pts
7. Oldhaven Wanderers	15	6	0	9	45	54	18
8. Heath Hill United	15	4	2	9	30	41	14
9. Lakeland Spurs	15	4	1	10	21	67	13
10. Kingsway Colts	**15**	**3**	**3**	**9**	**37**	**53**	**12**

Alfie already knew that following that day's game against Heath Hill, the Colts' last two matches were against third-placed Deansview Juniors and, finally, Oldhaven Wanderers.

While he was fairly confident that they could get a positive result against Oldhaven, who after winning their first five games of the season were now on a worse run of form than the Colts (in fact, they were the only team that Kingsway had managed to beat since Billy and

Hayden had left to join the Academy), he knew the Deansview game would be incredibly tough. Although they were unlikely to catch Ashgate at the top of the table, Deansview had every chance of overtaking Western Dynamos in second and getting promoted to division one.

"If we get four points from the next three games, then we'll be on 16 points," Alfie muttered to himself as he tried to work out a set of realistic results that would leave the Colts outside the bottom two. "Hopefully Lakeland and Heath Hill have got harder ends to the season than we have."

He used the mouse to roll the cursor

over Heath Hill's name and clicked the left button. The web page instantly brought up the team's final two remaining fixtures: Deansview Juniors and then Ashgate Athletic.

Alfie allowed himself a quick smile. 'There's no way they'll win either of those two games,' he thought smugly. 'If we beat them today and then get at least a draw against Oldhaven next week, then surely we'll finish above them.' His smile evaporated just seconds later, though, as he recalled just how confident he'd been about Lakeland Spurs not standing a chance of beating Ashgate seven days earlier.

Still, lightening couldn't strike twice. Could it?

Moving off Heath Hill's fixtures, Alfie clicked to bring up Lakeland's instead.

He bristled visibly as he noticed that Spurs were playing against Oldhaven later that day, before finishing against Brook Wanderers and Melrose Youth, who were in fifth and sixth place respectively.

Alfie could easily imagine Lakeland managing to pick up four points from those three games; an eventuality that would move them onto 17 points and mean that the Colts' would need at least two wins from their final three games to overtake them.

After running through a few other possible outcomes in his head, Alfie realised that he was only serving to make himself even more nervous. He knew deep down that the best thing he could do was to concentrate on the Colts' own games and forget about what the other teams did and didn't need to do. He was also only too aware that doing this was far easier said than done.

Switching off the computer, an anxious Alfie wandered back to his bedroom and picked up the teddy bear that he'd accidentally knocked off the shelf with Megan's magazine the previous evening.

When Madam Zola had given him the bear a couple of Christmases ago, she'd told him that it was lucky and would give him the one thing he really wanted. When he'd whispered to the bear a couple of weeks later that what he really wanted was Jimmy Grimshaw to replace Keith Johnson as coach of the Kingsway Colts this had happened.

He looked at the bear again. "Please help the Colts win today," he said to it, desperately hoping that Megan wouldn't enter his room and find him speaking to a cuddly toy. "And please make Madam Zola come and find me. I really need to speak to her."

With that, Alfie stuffed the bear into his football bag alongside his muddy football boots.

There were still two hours until Mr Walker was due to pick him up for the game.

Maybe, just maybe, that would be enough time for another meeting with Madam Zola.

Chapter eight

Kingsway's new coach, Scott Foreman, was a man of few words. His pre-match team talks tended to consist of little more than reading out the team and then wishing his players luck for the game ahead.

Prior to the Heath Hill match, though, the coach was far more vocal than usual.

"I really feel that we can get a win today," he declared confidently, as the Colts' squad huddled around him. "We were really unlucky to lose against this mob last time out. You controlled the game and created more than enough chances to win the game comfortably..."

"If I'd been there then you would definitely have won," interrupted Liam boastfully. He'd missed the last game between the two teams as Kingsway United had been playing at home on the same day and, as a season ticket holder, he'd decided to go and watch them instead.

Scott shot Liam a stern look. "We don't know that for definite, Liam. Just make sure you stick away any chances you get today or that boast may come back to haunt you later."

Liam blushed slightly, causing a few of his teammates to smile.

Turning to face the rest of the squad, Danny's Dad continued with his team-talk. "You've been playing fairly well all season, but at times we've given up too easily when we've fallen behind which, let's face it, has happened quite often. We don't do that today, though, okay! We keep going right until the final whistle, no matter what happens. You completely outplayed a very good Southfield side last week and even their coach said to me at the end of the game that you were unlucky not to have won. Play like that today and I'm certain you will win."

Alfie nodded enthusiastically, delighted to hear his coach being so positive. Glancing at his teammates, though, he couldn't help but feel that most of the other Colts' players weren't listening to a single word their coach was saying. They seemed to be more interested in pulling silly faces and trying to make each other laugh than they were on focussing on the important game ahead.

"The team today," continued Scott, "is Pranav in goal; Danny, Luke and Des in defence; Alfie on the left of midfield, Chloe and Isaac in the centre, and Will on the right. Liam is up front by himself, but I want the midfielders, especially you Alfie and Will, to get up and support him as often as possible. Be mindful that you still need to get back and defend too, though. Ollie, you're starting as sub, but you'll definitely get on for a good 20 minutes at least. Is that okay?"

"No worries," Ollie responded.

This was Ollie Sudbury's second season as a Colts player, but Alfie was fairly sure that he had absolutely no interest in football whatsoever. He was sub almost every week, yet this never seemed to bother Ollie in the slightest. Even when he did get to play, he just tended to stand rooted to the spot, watching the game go on around him.

Still, since the Colts' only other

registered player, Spencer Ramsey, had recently moved away from the Kingsway, area Ollie was the only option the team had, so he would have to do.

Scott added a few more words of encouragement, then wished the team good luck and told them to go and line up in their positions. A minute or so later the referee called the two captains into the centre circle for the coin toss and a short while later the game was underway.

As Madam Zola hadn't made an appearance prior to kick off, Alfie was hopeful that the other plea he'd made to his 'lucky' teddy bear earlier that morning would come true instead – that the Colts would finally record a long overdue victory.

Not that he was prepared to let the outcome of the match rely solely on a request made to a stuffed toy. He was determined to do everything he possibly could to help his team pick up an invaluable three points.

Just two minutes of the match had been played when Alfie won a crunching 50/50 tackle against a much larger opponent, got the ball under control and darted up the left wing with it. A Heath Hill defender moved across to close him down, but before he could get there, Alfie used the outside of his boot to flick the ball towards Isaac Lincoln, a player who had joined the Colts from Danehill United at the beginning of the season.

While Isaac tended to play in the position that Hayden had once occupied, he wasn't anywhere near as skilful as his predecessor had been. The one thing he could do better than Hayden, though, was strike a ball powerfully. Alfie believed that Isaac could blast a ball even harder than Jasper; the advantage being that when Isaac's foot connected with the ball, it usually went in the vague direction that he intended it to.

As the ball rolled towards Isaac from Alfie's pass, there was only one thing in the boy's mind. To shoot. He swung his right leg and smashed the ball with as much power as he could muster.

The ball zoomed through the air, but was heading a good distance wide before it whacked into Liam's backside. The ball spun in the air, changed direction and flew into the net, completely wrong-footing the Heath Hill goalkeeper. 1-0 to the Colts.

"Ouuucccchhhh," yelled Liam as his teammates ran towards him. It was hard to tell whether the delight on their faces had been caused by the Colts taking the lead or by their cocky friend's obvious discomfort.

"You're so lucky," chuckled Chloe, as she high-fived him.

"You call that lucky?" cried Liam. "My bum is in agony!"

All of the celebrating Colts' players laughed loudly. "I'm surprised you're not saying that you meant it," grinned Alfie.

"What are you talking about?" grimaced Liam as he rubbed gingerly at the spot where the ball had struck him. "Of course I meant it."

The smiles on the faces of the Colts' players didn't last for long, though. From their very first attack, Heath Hill equalised in as fortuitous fashion as which the Colts had taken the lead.

Under pressure from Liam, a Heath Hill defender toe-punted the ball up to the other end of the pitch, bypassing every outfield player. Initially unsure as to whether the ball had enough power on it to roll into his penalty box or not, Pranav hesitated momentarily before deciding to come out of his area to clear the ball with his feet.

Unfortunately, though, a Heath Hill

forward had chased after the ball and Pranav's brief hesitation had allowed the attacker to get closer to it than he should have. Although the goalkeeper just about reached the ball first, his attempted clearance merely struck the Heath Hill forward's body and rebounded over the stranded Pranav's head and into the goal. 1-1.

However, much to Scott Foreman's delight, his team responded far more positively to this latest misfortune than they had to conceding sloppy goals in previous weeks.

The Colts' stepped up their play; passing quickly, moving fluently and creating a host of goal scoring opportunities as the half-time whistle approached.

The best of Kingsway's numerous chances fell to Will Cassidy, a friend of Danny's who had joined the Colts when Billy was selected for the Academy. Once again Alfie was involved. The left midfielder sent over a cross aiming for Liam. Although the ball was just too high for the striker, it also eluded the Heath Hill centre back and fell invitingly for the inrushing Will at the far post.

Choosing to strike the ball first time, when taking a touch may have been a better option, Will's right boot failed to make a clean connection with the ball and the shot landed tamely into the arms of the grateful Heath Hill goalie.

Then, just before half-time, disaster struck.

Another long, hoofed clearance from a Heath Hill defender should have been headed clear by Danny. However, the talented defender hadn't shouted to let his teammates know that he was in control of the situation so Des had also risen to try and head the ball away from danger.

The two boys collided in mid-air, both missing the ball, much to the glee of the Heath Hill number 14 who suddenly found himself clean through on goal. The attacker took one touch to set himself and then smashed a right-footed shot past a helpless Pranav to give Heath Hill an entirely undeserved 2-1 lead.

Alfie sunk to his knees, scarcely able to believe what was happening.

He could see no possible way that the team could have performed any better than they had in the first half, yet they were still losing.

Despondently, Alfie walked back into his position, waiting for the ref to restart the game for the reaming few seconds of the first half.

He was so concerned about the fact that the Colts were losing again, that it took him a few seconds to realise he was the only Kingsway player standing in a position ready to restart the game.

Glancing over his shoulder to find out where the rest of his teammates were, Alfie was horrified to see his friends and Scott gathered around Danny, who was lying on the floor grasping his left knee.

He jogged quickly over to join his teammates and asked Chloe what was happening.

"He hurt his knee when he landed after trying to head the ball," she answered.

"Ahhhh. That really hurts, Dad!" screamed Danny, as Scott gently tried to straighten his son's leg.

"There's no way you can continue," said Scott ruefully. He looked over at Ollie, who was sat on the sideline paying undivided attention to a worm that had wriggled up through the broken soil. "Ollie," he called at the top of his voice. "Ollie. OLLIE!"

It took Scott and the rest of the Colts players another 30 seconds of shouting before they were able to rouse the sub's attention. "Get ready, Ollie," Scott yelled. "You're coming on for Danny."

Alfie could barely conceal a sigh of disappointment as Scott carried his injured son off the pitch and Ollie strolled onto it looking decidedly disinterested.

The Colts' chances of winning the match had just become a whole lot slimmer.

Chapter nine

As Scott tended to Danny during the
half-time break, the rest of the Colts'
players sat in a miserable silence, fearing
they were half-an-hour away from yet
another loss.

Alfie really wanted to deliver an
inspirational team talk; one that would
fire up his teammates and ultimately lead
them to the victory they so desperately
needed. But he was so gutted by the
way the first half had transpired that he
simply didn't know what to say. All he
could think about was the fact that if the
team couldn't somehow turn the game
around then it would almost certainly
mean the end of the Kingsway Colts.

To Alfie's immense surprise, it was

Liam who took it upon himself to lift the dejected Kingsway squad.

"Get your heads up everyone," he implored, standing up and clapping his hands together three times. "You heard what Scott said before the game, right?"

Most of the Colts' players stared blankly at one another and shrugged their shoulders, confirming Alfie's thoughts that few of his teammates had been paying any attention to their coach before the game.

"He told us that we have to keep going and play to the final whistle. No matter what happens," Alfie replied, as it became apparent that no one else knew the answer.

"That's right," Liam declared. "So that's exactly what we do. I don't know about you lot, but I'm fed up with losing every week. We're better than them," he gestured in the direction of the Heath Hill players. "A lot better. But there's no way that we'll win this game until we start believing in ourselves more."

A few of the Colts' players murmured without enthusiasm. It was clear that none of them truly believed they could come back... not without Danny.

"Look, if you don't think we can win,

then we may as well give up and go home now," Liam continued, the anger in his voice steadily growing. "Some of you may know that I've been asked to play for Ashgate Athletic next season, and I know that some of you are also thinking about leaving." He glanced pointedly at Chloe, while Alfie turned his attentions to Des and Luke. "But right now I'm a Colts player, and while I play for this team I'm going to do all I can to help us win this game. If you don't think we can win, just get up and go now."

No one moved.

"Now come on then," Liam roared. "Let's get out there and win this game." He looked sideways to where Scott was encouraging his son to try and walk. "Let's win it for Danny," he added.

"Come on boys," Chloe shouted. "Let's do this!"

"Let's go Colts" Pranav yelled.

Suddenly all the Colts' players were on their feet, shouting loudly and looking a million times more animated than they had only a few seconds earlier. Well, all except for Ollie, who was still searching for the worm that had kept him so captivated during the first half.

"Nice one, Liam," Alfie said as the two

friends walked back on to the pitch.

"Thank me later," Liam replied. "We've got a game to win."

In spite of Liam's motivational team talk, the opening ten minutes of the second half were the most even of the match. Isaac spurned a good chance to level, shooting high over the bar from close range, while Pranav made two good saves to stop Heath Hill extending their lead.

While the Colts were still playing well, they were clearly missing Danny's assured presence and leadership qualities. The fact was that, with Ollie on the pitch, they may as well have been playing with eight players. He just didn't move or show any desire to get involved in the game whatsoever.

It was something that the Health Hill players – or at least their coach – had clearly noticed. Time after time they aimed their attacks in Ollie's direction, seemingly well aware of the fact that the Colts' substitute probably wouldn't be paying much attention to what was going on. Des and Luke had to work overtime in order to cover for him.

However, in a clear reversal of what had happened in the first half, with just under ten minutes of the game left, the Colts' equalised following a sustained period of Health Hill pressure.

Chloe won the ball in the centre circle and went on a surging run through the middle of the pitch. As they'd been instructed to do so at the beginning of the game, Will and Alfie bombed forward to try and offer support to Liam and give Chloe some extra options. Their presence distracted two of Heath Hill's defenders, both of whom were unsure as to whether they should close down Chloe or stay where they were so they could cover the wide players should she choose to pass.

"Close her down," screamed the third defender, who was marking Liam, as Chloe advanced into shooting range.

As one, both defenders rushed towards Chloe, but the Colts' midfielder didn't panic. She calmly feigned a pass left to Alfie, before instead threading the ball to the right where Will was running. Will was through on goal and was just about to shoot when his earlier missed effort flashed through his mind. Losing confidence in his ability to score, he elected to pass the ball square to Liam.

The Colts' striker, as ever sensing the chance of a goal, had anticipated that

Will might pass and reached the ball just ahead of his marker, lashing it first-time high into the net, out of reach of the goalkeeper. 2-2.

Unusually for Liam, he chose not to celebrate the goal, instead running to retrieve the ball so that the game could be restarted as quickly as possible.

From that point on, the momentum of the game swung back in Kingsway's favour as they launched wave after wave of attack on the Heath Hill goal. The opposition stood firm, though, restricting the Colts' players to mainly long-range efforts.

Then, with just two minutes of the match left, another perfectly weighted pass from Chloe sent Alfie through on goal. Working the ball onto his favoured left foot, Alfie whacked the ball hard and low, aiming for a gap that the Heath Hill 'keeper had left at his near post.

The shot didn't quite have the required accuracy. The ball smashed against the post only to then rebound off the diving goalkeeper's back and head once more in the direction of the goal.

It seemed to take an age for the ball to cross the line but when it finally did, much to Alfie's despair, it rolled the wrong side of the post, missing the target by mere inches.

There was no time for anguish, though. Immediately, Alfie rushed behind the goal to get the ball for the resulting corner. He carefully placed it on the ground and took a deep breath to compose himself. If ever there was a time that he needed to produce a perfect delivery, this was it.

Every Kingsway player with the exception of Pranav, who was standing on the halfway line, was inside the Heath Hill penalty area. Alfie began his run up and sent the ball across, desperate for one of his teammates to get on the end of it. The delivery was perfect. Des rose above his marker and headed the ball powerfully goalwards.

For the second time in less than a minute, the Colts' players and supporters were sure that they had scored. For the second time in less than a minute, though, they were denied by the woodwork, this time the ball thudding off the crossbar.

All of the Colts players flung their hands on their heads, unable to believe their bad luck.

Well... all except for one.

The ball landed at Ollie's feet – none

of the Heath Hill players had bothered to mark him, not deeming him to be any threat whatsoever. Seemingly paying little attention to what was going on around him, Ollie flicked his leg absent-mindedly at the ball, sending it past the disbelieving Heath Hill goalkeeper.

For a second no one moved.

Then, as one, all of the Colts' players, aside from a still stunned Ollie who remained rooted to the spot, roared in celebration, while Danny, Scott and all of the watching parents cheered loudly from the sideline.

A second or two later, finally realising what had happened, Ollie started jumping up and down, excitedly waving his arms around in the air whilst yelling "I've scored, I've scored!" in a tone that confirmed that he was just as shocked by what he'd just done as everyone else was.

Ollie was still smiling broadly moments later when the referee blew his whistle to end the match.

The contrast between the two teams as they left the pitch was stark. The Kingsway players celebrated their first win for nine games as though they had won the league, while the Heath Hill players trudged despondently in

the direction of their parents' cars,
still unable to believe what had just
happened.

The Colts' hopes of escaping relegation
were still alive thanks to the unlikeliest
of heroes.

Chapter ten

Alfie's buoyant mood didn't last for long.

Later that evening, sitting once again in front of his parents' computer, his earlier fears that Lakeland Spurs would probably beat Oldhaven Wanderers were confirmed.

However, while Alfie had suspected that Lakeland may well win against Oldhaven, the margin of their victory came as a shock.

"5-1!" Alfie exclaimed aloud, clearly surprised that Spurs had won the game so comprehensively.

Alfie felt a knot tightening in his stomach. Having beaten Ashgate last Sunday and Oldhaven so comfortably today, Lakeland, it seemed, were starting to find form at exactly the right time – or the wrong time, depending on your point of view.

Even though he already knew that this result would mean the Colts were still in the bottom two, Alfie decided to bring up the updated league table anyway.

His eyes fell straight away to the bottom three places.

8. Lakeland Spurs	16	5	1	10	26	68	16
9. Kingsway Colts	**16**	**4**	**3**	**9**	**40**	**55**	**15**
10. Heath Hill United	16	4	2	10	32	44	14

'At least we're not last anymore,' he brooded, trying his hardest to be positive.

If the Lakeland result had taken some of the gloss off Alfie's good mood following the Colts' triumph over Heath Hill, then the sheen was wiped away completely within minutes of him arriving at school the following morning.

Alfie had barely walked into the classroom alongside Billy when he spotted something that made him groan loudly.

Towards the back of the classroom, Danny was sitting on a chair. Although he was being partially surrounded by Hayden, Chloe, Liam and Pranav, Alfie

noticed immediately that his teammate's
right leg was elevated on another chair.
Just behind him, leant against the back
wall, was a pair of crutches.

Alfie hurried over to his teammate, with
Billy following close behind. "How bad
is it?" he asked, gesturing towards his
friend's knee.

"The doctor said I've probably torn some
ligaments, although there's too much
swelling to tell just how bad it is at the
moment," Danny answered flatly.

"Oh no way, that's terrible. Does it
hurt?" Billy enquired.

"Not really," Danny replied. "Not now
anyway. It really, really hurt yesterday,

when I did it. We were in hospital for hours. It was so boring! I did get to have an x-ray done, though, which was pretty cool, I suppose."

"Ooohhh no way," Alfie moaned, in a manner which made it sound like he was the one that was hurt rather than Danny. "Will you still be able to play on Sunday?" he asked, more in hope than expectation.

Danny laughed bitterly. "No Alfie. The doctor said I won't be kicking a football until the summer at least. Probably not until next season. If it's really bad then... who knows?"

Without so much as another word, Alfie slunk away to his own desk, reeling from the news that the Colts' best defender wouldn't be available for the team's two remaining matches.

He was only too aware that this turn of events would leave Scott Foreman with no other choice but to start Ollie for the games against Oldhaven Wanderers and Deansview Juniors.

While one of the major advantages to the Kingsway Colts having a small squad may have been that he got to play a full game almost every week, not for the first time that season, Alfie found himself reflecting on the flip side to this benefit.

Namely, when someone was unavailable to play, it significantly weakened the team; especially since Hayden and Billy had been called up to the Kingsway United Academy and Spencer had moved away.

Alfie was still consumed by thoughts of how the Colts would be able to overcome this latest problem when his teacher marched into the classroom and ordered the children to go and sit at their own desks.

"Do you think you could have been a little bit more sympathetic?" Billy asked, as he plonked himself down in the seat next to Alfie.

Alfie looked confused, "What do you mean?"

"You didn't ask Danny how he was feeling... wish him a speedy recovery... or anything like that," Billy admonished. "You basically sounded like all you wanted to know was whether he'd be able to play on Sunday or not. When he said he couldn't, you just walked away."

Alfie was just about to angrily refute Billy's accusations when he suddenly realised that what his best friend was saying was correct. The truth was that he hadn't given a moment's thought to how Danny must be feeling about being hurt and unable to play a game he loved for a few months. All he'd been concerned about was how Danny's injury would negatively affect the Colts.

He glanced over at where Danny was sitting. It was fair to say that his friend looked utterly miserable, even though he was obviously trying his best to put a brave face on the situation in front of the other children.

"You're right Billy," Alfie replied guiltily. "I'll go and apologise to him at break time."

Feelings of guilt continued to gnaw away at Alfie throughout the whole of that morning's lesson. So much so that, instead of listening to his teacher as she tried to prepare the class for the forthcoming end-of-Year 6 exams, all Alfie could think about was why he had acted so selfishly towards Danny.

The more he thought about it, the more he became convinced that the blame lay with one person and one person only: Madam Zola.

If it wasn't for her telling him that he had to stay with the Colts in order to ensure his destiny of one day becoming a professional footballer came true, then the outcome of the Colts' final two games of the season wouldn't seem anywhere near as important as they currently did.

Sure, Alfie would undoubtedly be extremely sad if the Colts were to get relegated, and he'd be sadder still if this was to lead to the team folding. But what he was really worried about was that, if these two things did happen, then his dream of becoming a professional footballer wouldn't come true.

It was this that had made the idea of finishing in the bottom two positions so entirely unthinkable for him.

What Alfie really found frustrating, though, was that he wasn't even sure whether the warning the fortune teller had given him more than two years earlier was still relevant or not.

Would it matter if the Colts were to fold? Would this really put an end to his dream?

'It's all Madam Zola's fault,' Alfie grumbled silently to himself as, in the background, his teacher outlined some of the maths questions he and his classmates could expect to face in the approaching exams. 'Why won't she just visit me and tell me what I need to know?'

He looked over at Danny again and felt a fresh wave of guilt wash over him. There was absolutely no doubt in his mind that it was Madam Zola's fault that he'd acted so inconsiderately towards his friend and teammate.

It was at that moment that he decided there was only one thing for it.

If she wasn't going to come to him, then he'd have to find her.

Chapter eleven

Over the course of the next few days, Alfie spent hours visiting some of the spots in which he'd previously met Madam Zola, hoping that he'd be fortunate enough to catch a glimpse of her again.

His search took him to Megan's old infant school, the Kingsway Shopping Mall, Ashgate Community Park, the Danehill Woods... he even visited the local DVD hire shop so that he could re-hire a DVD that he'd been watching when Madam Zola had suddenly appeared on his television screen.

Although Alfie's Mum was more than a little confused by her son's sudden urgency to visit all of these seemingly random locations, he'd been so insistent about his need to do so that she had eventually agreed to drive him to each place.

Mrs Jones' feelings of bafflement only further increased when Alfie asked her if she would mind taking him to all of the shops in the local area which sold wind chimes.

Many of his past meetings with Madam Zola had been preceded by the sound of wind chimes chiming, so he figured that maybe if he went to a shop that sold them, then he might possibly see the fortune teller there.

After spending a considerable length of time begging his Mum to take him to the particular shops, a slightly bewildered Mrs Jones once again relented and agreed to assist her son with his rather bizarre demands.

She soon wished she hadn't.

In every shop they visited, much to Mrs Jones' immense embarrassment and the staff's general annoyance, Alfie insisted on flicking all of the wind chimes to make them jangle. Having run out of ideas of what else he could do to hasten a meeting with Madam Zola, Alfie hoped, rather optimistically it has to be said, that maybe, just maybe, the sound of a load

of wind chimes chiming at the same time
would somehow summon her to him.

Yet, no matter where he looked, or what
he tried, not once did he catch sight of
anyone who even vaguely resembled the
mysterious old fortune teller.

By the morning of the Oldhaven game,
Alfie's search for Madam Zola had yielded
only more frustration and had done
nothing whatsoever to ease his mind
ahead of the match.

As had been the case a week earlier,
he'd hardly slept a wink during the night
prior to the game, and once again he
found himself awake extremely early on a
Sunday morning.

Alfie got changed into his blue Kingsway kit, made sure that his football boots were in his boot bag and then sat back on his bed. He considered turning on the TV to watch the previous day's football highlights, but then realised it was so early that the programme hadn't actually even started yet.

He flung himself backwards on to his bed and stared up at the ceiling, trying desperately to think about anything other than Madam Zola or that day's match against Oldhaven. Within seconds, tiredness overwhelmed him and he fell into a comfortable sleep, coming to a couple of hours later when he heard someone knocking on his bedroom door.

"Alfie, are you awake sweetie?" Mrs Jones called softly. "Liam and his Dad will be here any minute to take you to the game. I thought you were already awake. I heard you banging about earlier and thought you were getting dressed."

"I was. Be there in a minute Mum," Alfie replied, trying his best to hide the tiredness from his voice.

Checking the clock on his wall, a bleary-eyed and somewhat disorientated Alfie realised to his surprise that he must have fallen back asleep. He jumped off his bed, grabbed his 'lucky' teddy bear from the shelf and, for the umpteenth time that week, begged it to bring Madam Zola to him. Then, almost as an afterthought, he also asked the bear to bring the Colts' luck for the Oldhaven game, before stuffing it into his boot bag.

Zipping the bag shut, Alfie was just about to sit back on his bed when he heard a car horn beeping close by.

"Liam and his Dad are here, Alf" Mr Jones shouted from downstairs.

Alfie rushed out of his room and was just about to slam the door shut behind him when he noticed that there was something pinned to it.

Pausing momentarily to examine what it was, he sighed heavily and rolled his eyes as, upon closer inspection, he realised it was another one of Mystic Jane Folies' horoscope pages that had been neatly ripped out of one of Megan's magazines.

He had no idea why his sister had bothered to pin the page to his bedroom door and at that moment he didn't particularly care either. Tearing the page off the door, Alfie crumpled it into a ball and tossed it into the kitchen bin as he hurriedly grabbed a drink from the fridge before rushing outside to get into Mr Walker's car, shouting a hasty goodbye to his parents as he went.

"What has happened to your hair?" Liam laughed as Alfie climbed into the back seat alongside him. Alfie had been in such a rush to get out of the house that his blond curly hair, usually a mess at the best of times, was in a complete state from where he'd not had time to style it.

"My new look," Alfie grinned, before discreetly checking his hair in Mr Walker's rear-view mirror, realising just how messy it looked and then spending the rest of the journey trying to flatten it down without Liam noticing.

"Confident today boys?" Mr Walker asked, shortly before they arrived at the Kingsway Recreation Ground.

"I think so," Liam answered, nodding positively. "Oldhaven are on a really bad run of form. I think we'll win quite easily to be honest. What do you think Alfie?"

"Hopefully... maybe," Alfie replied uncertainly.

A week ago Alfie had been fully confident that the Colts would be able to beat Oldhaven. However, since learning of Danny's injury on Monday, he'd been unable to shake from his mind the fear that Ollie's involvement in the game would severely harm the team's chances of getting the win they so desperately needed, no matter how much he tried to be positive.

And as Mr Walker turned his car onto the gravel which served as Kingsway Recreation Ground's car park, Alfie knew that he was just over an hour away from discovering whether this fear would be realised.

Chapter twelve

It was a shocking decision. Alfie had no doubts about that whatsoever.

He was certain that he'd been well behind the last defender when Isaac had passed the ball through to him. In fact, he was equally positive that the parent who was running the line hadn't even bothered to raise his flag until after the ball had hit the back of the net.

Alfie had already sprinted off to celebrate the goal with his teammates, and was even contemplating performing a celebratory somersault – or at least attempting one – when he noticed that the referee was embroiled in a heated discussion with the linesperson; a father of one of the Oldhaven players.

At first, Alfie wasn't too concerned. Surely the referee would have noticed that he'd been well onside when the ball had been passed forward.

That the parent appeared to be so angry at having his decision scrutinised by the referee – he was theatrically waving his flag around in the air whilst agitatedly hopping up and down on the spot – was taken by Alfie as further proof that the ref was set to award the goal.

However, as the discussion between the referee and the parent had dragged on and on, the man holding the flag had become significantly calmer and Alfie had started to fear the worst. The ref was much younger than the parent, probably not that much older than the players themselves, and Alfie could see that he was visibly intimidated by the raging adult.

After deliberating with the linesperson for about a minute – even though it seemed like a lot longer to Alfie – the referee eventually turned away from him, blew his whistle and then loudly shouted, "No goal. Number 11 was offside."

Alfie was so disappointed – and shocked – by the decision, that he was rendered momentarily speechless.

With only a few minutes of the first half remaining the score should have been 2-0 to the Colts. Instead, it was still only 1-0, courtesy of a goal that had been scored by Liam midway through the first half.

Had Alfie's goal been allowed to stand, then it would have been just reward for a first half in which Kingsway had been by far and away the dominant team. Oldhaven had yet to muster a single shot on target and, while the Colts hadn't created oodles of clear goal scoring opportunities, they had nevertheless controlled the game and looked a far more threatening attacking side than their opposition.

So far, Alfie's fears about Ollie's involvement in the game had proved completely unfounded. Even though it was fair to say that he, along with Des and Luke in the Colts' defence, hadn't had much to do, on the few occasions that Oldhaven had attempted to launch an attack, Ollie had been alert enough to get his body in the way to at least make things difficult for the Wanderers' forwards.

Alfie was still seething about his disallowed goal when he suddenly found the ball at his feet again a few moments later. Feeding off the adrenaline that was still pumping through his body as a result of the injustice he believed he'd just suffered, Alfie went on a determined run towards the Oldhaven goal.

He swiftly evaded a couple of challenges as he burst into the opponents' penalty area. Glancing up, he instantly realised that he was in a great position to shoot and was just pulling his left leg back to do so when, in an attempt to put him under pressure, one of the chasing defenders accidentally tapped his standing foot with their boot. Although the contact was minimal, Alfie had been moving at such a pace that even the briefest touch from his opponent was enough to send him tumbling to the grass.

The referee blew his whistle. "Penalty," he called, without a moment's hesitation.

"That's absolute rubbish ref," screamed the Oldhaven linesperson immediately. "He never touched him!"

The young ref looked across at the parent and for a moment Alfie feared that he was about to change his mind. Fortunately he didn't. "Penalty," he repeated, albeit not as convincingly as he had said it the first time.

"You don't know what you're doing

ref," the man holding the flag yelled. "Clueless. Absolutely clueless!" Alfie could not remember having ever seen anyone look so angry on the side of a football pitch before. Not even Keith Johnson!

Even the defender accused of committing the foul – who turned out to be the man's son – tried to calm him down, admitting that he had in fact made contact with Alfie's leg. But the boy's Dad wasn't having any of it. "Don't be so silly son," he fumed. "You don't have to make excuses for him. It's a terrible decision and that's that."

Eventually some of the other Oldhaven player's parents, along with the team's coach, managed to calm the man down enough to stop him from barracking the ref more, although he refused point blank to hand over the linesperson's flag to anyone else.

Once the kerfuffle had finally died down, Liam grabbed the ball and placed it carefully on the penalty spot. Alfie had hoped that his friend would let him take the spot kick, but he wasn't at all surprised when the Colts' leading scorer declined his request. There was no way Liam would ever give up a clear goal scoring chance and even Scott Foreman had called for the striker to take it with the game still so finely balanced.

Confidently, Liam stepped up and drove the ball hard and low into the bottom right-hand corner of the goal, well beyond the reach of the Oldhaven goalies' outstretched arm. 2-0.

The Colts' players all bundled on top of Liam, barely unable to conceal their joy at having doubled their lead. Alfie couldn't help but sneak a quick peek at the Oldhaven linesperson. He was still glaring at the referee, angrily shaking his head from side to side.

The penalty was the last meaningful action of the first half.

During the half-time break the Colts' players all gathered around Scott, swigging greedily from water bottles as they listened to what their coach had to say.

It was immediately clear that Scott was less than impressed with the behaviour of Oldhaven's linesperson.

"What an absolute numpty," Kingsway's coach exclaimed as he stared irritably in the direction of the still ranting parent, who had marched over to the referee to continue his vocal protestations regarding the penalty decision the moment the half-time whistle had sounded.

For a moment Scott considered going over to put a stop to the man's harassment of the poor young official. While Scott himself could get worked up by refereeing decisions from time to time, he also appreciated that the majority of youth football refs were little more than children themselves. Without them there wouldn't be anywhere near close to enough officials available to take charge of matches each week, so he always attempted to keep any frustrations he had hidden.

In addition, he had learned from Jimmy Grimshaw that it was essential for coaches to stay disciplined at all times in order to set a good example to their team. Being unsure as to whether or not he'd be able to keep his temper in check if he were to confront the still moaning Oldhaven parent, he ultimately decided that a more sensible course of action would be to steer clear and concentrate on his own team.

With a considerable effort, Kingsway's coach turned his attention away from the ref and his tormentor and focussed instead on the children crowded around him. "Great half," he started. "You're by far the better side and if you keep playing like you are then the only team that's going to win this match is you. Just keep doing exactly what you're doing."

Scott took a deep breath and glanced quickly in the direction of the Oldhaven parent who was still talking to the ref. The two had now been joined by the Wanderers' coach, who appeared to be urging the other man to apologise to the official.

"Look," continued Scott, concentrating once again on his players, "there's not really an awful lot I can say on what you can do to improve. As I've already said, more of the same please."

The Colts' players all nodded their agreement and, believing that there was no more to be added, were just about to head back onto the pitch when Scott stopped them. "One thing to be aware of, though," he began in a cautionary tone. "The ref has had a lot of pressure put on him by that..." he paused looking for a child-friendly way of saying what he wanted to say. "By that... wally, so it wouldn't surprise me if you get a few decisions go against you this half. The ref is only young and he may not even realise that he's doing it, but that... numpty, may have intimidated him to the point where he gives Oldhaven some dodgy decisions just to stop him from moaning. If it does happen, then don't moan at the ref. Just get your heads up and get on with the game."

With their coach's warning still ringing in their ears, the Colts' players retook to the pitch, every single one of them still fully confident that they were little more than half-an-hour away from claiming yet another vital three points.

However, none of them could have guessed just how accurate their coach's warning would prove to be.

Chapter thirteen

Barely five minutes of the second half had been played when the first decision went against the Colts.

Chloe had been clattered into inside the Oldhaven penalty area by the same defender who had fouled Alfie to give away the penalty in the first-half. But to the disbelief of every Kingsway player the referee waved play-on.

"You should book her for diving ref," screamed the opposition linesperson, as Chloe rolled around on the floor in a considerable amount of pain, the start of a bruise already beginning to form on her left knee where she'd been kicked.

Thankfully, although extremely sore, the injury wasn't too bad and she was soon able to continue, fuming silently at the ref's refusal to award a penalty – and even more angry at the accusation that she'd dived when she so clearly hadn't.

Chloe's blood was still boiling a few minutes later when she unwisely allowed her frustrations to get the better of her. Carelessly losing possession just outside her own area, she swung her leg in a vain attempt to regain the ball from the player who had dispossessed her.

The attempted tackle was clumsy at best, and Chloe could have no arguments when the ref blew his whistle for a free kick.

What she could have arguments about, though, was the fact that the referee then pointed to the penalty spot. "Penalty," he stated decisively.

"What?" Chloe shrieked loudly, unable to believe what was happening. "That was nowhere near inside the penalty area!"

She was right, too. The contact had been made a good two or three yards outside the area but the Oldhaven player's momentum had led to him rolling into the penalty box, and this was enough to convince the ref to give a spot kick.

Chloe, Alfie and Liam all ran over to

the official and were just about to angrily remonstrate further with him when they heard Scott's voice from the sideline. "Leave it you three," he shouted, although the frustration he himself felt was clearly audible from his tone. "Remember what I said at half-time. Just get on with the game and leave the ref alone."

Perhaps unsurprisingly, Oldhaven's linesperson didn't find anything to gripe about with this particular decision. "Great call, ref," he acknowledged loudly. "About time you gave us something."

The Oldhaven number eight picked the ball up and put it down on the spot.

"Come on Pranav," shouted Chloe, before all her teammates joined in with roaring words of encouragement to their goalkeeper.

The Oldhaven number eight stepped up and struck the penalty to Pranav's left. The shot was nowhere near as well struck as Liam's earlier effort had been and Pranav correctly guessed the way the striker would shoot. The Colts' goalkeeper got both of his hands to the ball and managed to firmly push it away from the goal.

"Justice," shouted Chloe.

"Great save, Pran," yelled Alfie.

Unfortunately for the Colts, though, the ball landed right at the feet of one of the other Oldhaven players who had advanced into the area while the Kingsway players had been celebrating their goalkeeper's save. With no one close to him, the Wanderers' player had plenty of time to control the ball and smash it into the empty net to reduce the deficit for his team. 2-1.

"Forget about that. Just keep doing what you were doing in the first half," Scott called encouragingly from the sideline.

However, for the next few minutes the goal seemed to galvanise Oldhaven and they began to have their best spell of the match, putting the Colts defence under near-constant pressure, albeit without creating any clear-cut shooting opportunities.

Alfie was starting to feel increasingly concerned that Kingsway would end up throwing the game away if they weren't careful. It was clear to him that some of his teammates had let the injustice of the earlier decisions get to them – Chloe and Des in particular.

They had taken to muttering under their breath every time the ref gave a decision, either to sarcastically agree with the call or to further berate him. This had started to affect the performance of both players – and indeed the rest of the team – who were now putting more effort into moaning than they were to playing.

Realising that the Colts' were in desperate need of a third goal in order to settle their growing frustrations, Alfie used a combination of speed, skill and guile to bring the ball out of defence and launch a counter attack. Moving rapidly towards the halfway line he played a perfectly timed one-two with Liam and received the ball back deep in opposition territory, with just two defenders left to beat.

Although Alfie could see Will steaming up the right wing in plenty of space, he had already decided that he was going to go for goal himself. Cutting inside the challenge of the first defender, he immediately struck the ball with the laces of his left boot, drilling it hard and low across the face of the goal.

The ball flew past the 'keeper, and would have smashed satisfyingly into the back of the net were it not for the outstretched leg of the second Oldhaven defender preventing it from crossing the line.

Fortunately, Will had not stopped his burst forward, even when it had become clear that Alfie had no intention of passing to him. The defender's clearance bounced straight into Will's chest and trickled over the line. 3-1... or so the Colts' player's initially thought.

Once again, the Oldhaven linesperson had his flag raised.

"There's no way that he can be offside ref," an exasperated Scott shouted from the sideline. "Their last defender was on the goal-line."

For the second time in the match the ref entered into a long discussion with the flag waving Oldhaven parent.

'Surely there's no way he can disallow the goal this time,' Alfie thought to himself. 'Will was even more clearly onside than I was.'

He was wrong.

"No goal," the ref shouted a few seconds later. "Number seven used his hand to push the ball into the net."

The Kingsway players simply couldn't believe it. Will ran over to the official, lifting his shirt to show off a red mark where the ball had struck his chest, while the rest of the players made their displeasure very clear.

Even Scott was moaning angrily from the side of the pitch, until he remembered his earlier advice and then began ordering his team to get off the ref's back and get on with the game.

"Sorry boys," explained the Oldhaven linesperson, not sounding at all sorry. "I can only give what I see."

Alfie could have sworn that he saw the sliest of smiles cross the linesperson's face momentarily, although when he looked again the parent was doing his best to look as earnest as possible.

Yet if the lineperson hoped that his latest involvement in the game would further knock the Colts' confidence, then he couldn't have been more wrong. This time, each and every Kingsway player took their frustrations out in completely the right way, lifting their performances to a level that even exceeded their first-half's showing.

The ball rarely left the Oldhaven half for the next ten minutes, but in spite of further attempts from Alfie, Isaac and Liam, the Colts' just couldn't snatch that all-important third goal.

With five minutes left, Kingsway

were running out of ideas on what they could do to break down their resolute opponents. Will and Alfie began crossing the ball at every opportunity, hoping that if they got the ball into the box enough then eventually it would fall for one of their teammates to have a clear chance on goal and put the game out of Oldhaven's reach.

It was a cross from Will that was to ultimately lead to the next goal.

Having tricked his way past two Wanderers' players, Will sent over a cross aiming towards the far post where Alfie was lurking with intent. Not for the first time, though, it was an Oldhaven defender who reached the ball first and managed to head it powerfully clear.

The ball bounced towards the halfway line where Ollie was the furthest player back for the Colts.

With time and space, Ollie had a number of options available to him. Chloe was in space a little to his right. Liam was pointing to where he had spotted a gap between two Oldhaven defenders if Ollie could manage to squeeze the ball through to him. The ball had bounced so invitingly that Ollie could even have attempted a long range shot himself

– as ambitious as a strike from such a distance would have been.

Instead he did none of those things. In fact he didn't do anything.

The Colts had been so on top in the later stages of the game, that Des and Luke had pushed further and further forward, leaving Ollie at the back on his own with very little to do. Standing there bored, Ollie's mind had drifted momentarily onto other things and it was only when he heard a panicking Alfie call his name that he remembered what it was that he was supposed to be doing.

But by then it was too late.

Before Ollie had a chance to move, the furthest forward Oldhaven player had reached the ball and knocked it into the Colts' half where only Pranav was standing.

Ollie turned to give chase and managed to catch up with the Wanderers' player just as he entered the Colts' penalty area. The Oldhaven player had run a long way with the ball and was breathing heavily as Ollie pulled up alongside him. He went to shoot but lost balance as he did so, toeing the ball harmlessly into Pranav's arms before stumbling to the floor.

Ollie breathed a huge sigh of relief as

Pranav drop-kicked the ball back upfield away from danger.

It was only then that the ref blew his whistle.

"Penalty," he shouted for the third time in the match. "Foul by number 14."

"Yessss," shouted the Oldhaven linesperson, before adding, "Now send him off ref. He was the last man."

If there was a silver lining for Ollie, it was that at least the ref ignored this advice.

Yet again the Kingsway players crowded around the ref, incensed by the decision. This time it took all of Scott's powers of self control, which were by now being tested to the very limit, not to take issue with the referee and eventually he composed himself enough to get his players to calm down.

It was second time lucky for the Oldhaven number eight who, correctly guessing that Pranav would dive the same way as he had earlier, blasted the ball straight down the middle of the goal to equalise for the Wanderers. 2-2.

Each and every Kingsway player was left clearly deflated by the goal. The remaining five minutes of the game belonged to Oldhaven who would have won the match with the very last kick of the game, were it not for a fantastic save from Pranav.

At full-time Scott marched angrily over to confront the Oldhaven linesperson, who strenuously denied cheating at any point during the game. The Colts players themselves had all slumped to the floor, unable to comprehend how they had not won the game. They all felt utterly cheated.

Ollie was in floods of tears, blaming himself for the Oldhaven equaliser, and nothing that his teammates or Scott said to him could make him feel any better.

Alfie himself was fighting back the tears. As he knelt on the ground, rubbing at his eyes, he realised only too well that if Lakeland Spurs had managed to beat Brook Wanderers then Kingsway would be relegated.

The linesperson's unfair decisions, combined with his influence over the young referee, could possibly have led to the end of the Kingsway Colts.

Chapter fourteen

The Colts' hopes of avoiding relegation were still alive. Just.

Alfie didn't even have to wait for the results to be uploaded onto the Middleton District Youth League website that Sunday evening to discover that Lakeland Spurs had drawn 3-3 with Brook Wanderers.

Jimmy Grimshaw had gone to watch the match as there were a couple of Brook Wanderers players who the Kingsway United Academy were keeping tabs on. As soon as Jimmy had got home from the game he'd phoned Scott Foreman to tell him the score. Scott had then told Danny who had promptly texted all of his teammates the good news.

Alfie had been sitting on his bed, still feeling utterly dejected following that morning's match, when he heard his mobile phone vibrate on his bedside table. He couldn't stop himself from letting out a huge cheer, if not of delight than certainly of relief, as he read the message.

The sudden excitable outburst brought Megan to his room.

"What are you so happy about?" she asked, as she skipped playfully over to her brother's bed, skilfully avoiding the various bits and bobs that were scattered all over the carpet.

"Lakeland Spurs drew with Brook Wanderers," he replied excitedly.

"Big wow," Megan responded, completely disinterestedly. Like her parents, Megan had absolutely no interest in football whatsoever. She couldn't even begin to understand what Alfie found so fascinating about chasing a ball around a muddy field. "I thought it must have been something interesting... like a message from your girlfriend, Chloe."

Alfie chose to ignore his sister. Megan was always trying to wind him up by saying that Chloe was his girlfriend, and

116

the more he tried to explain to his sibling that she was just a friend who happened to be a girl, the more Megan would go on and on about him being in love with his teammate. Over time he'd learned that the best course of action was to simply say ignore her and say nothing at all.

Realising that her brother wasn't going to respond to her wind-up attempts, Megan let out a heavy sigh of frustration and turned to leave the room.

Just before she got to the door, though, Alfie remembered that he had something he wanted to ask his sister about.

"By the way, moggy, why did you pin a page from one of your magazines to my bedroom door this morning?"

Megan spun on her heels to face Alfie, a look of pure anger on her face. "Don't call me moggy," she moaned. "You know I hate it when you call me that. If you do it again I'm telling Mum and Dad."

"Tell them then," Alfie dared her. "I'll just tell them that you've been pinning things to my bedroom door to try and annoy me."

Megan continued to glare angrily at her brother for a moment, before in the blink of an eye her expression turned from one of fury to confusion. "Wait a minute...

I didn't pin anything on your door this morning."

Now it was Alfie's turn to let out a deep sigh. "Yes you did Megan. It was a page from one of your magazines. The horoscopes page by that Jane Folies, or whatever her name is. I threw it in the bin. I've told you before that I don't believe in all that rubbish."

The look of bafflement on Megan's face only further intensified as her brother continued to talk. Begrudgingly, Alfie had to admit that his sister was certainly a good actress. "It wasn't me," she declared defiantly. "Why would I bother doing that?"

"I don't know," Alfie answered, nonchalantly shrugging his shoulders. "No doubt there was something written on the page that was supposed to have annoyed me. Well it didn't work, because I threw it away before I even read it. So unless you tell me, I guess I'll never know."

"How can I tell you what it was supposed to have said when I don't even know what you're talking about?" She certainly sounded well and truly outraged by the accusations her older brother was making, and Alfie once again had to concede just how convincing she was being. Not that he believed her protestations of innocence for a second.

"Okay then," he continued, smugly. "If it really wasn't you, go and get your newest magazine and show me the horoscopes page."

"Why should I?"

"To prove the page is still there, which, of course, it won't be, because you ripped it out and pinned it to my door this morning!"

"I don't have to prove anything to you," Megan yelled, before once again turning away from Alfie and stomping out of his room.

Alfie chuckled to himself as he listened to his younger sister's footsteps echo all the way down the hallway, followed moments later by the sound of her bedroom door slamming shut.

There was a part of Alfie that was curious to know just what Jane Folies had written that had prompted Megan to pin the page to his door.

Briefly, he considered fishing the crumpled page out of the kitchen bin, but knowing that all the unfinished food from lunch time had since been scraped into it, he quickly decided against doing so.

He was confident that he'd find out
what had been written on the page sooner
or later anyway. Megan had never been
very good at keeping secrets for long.

Chapter fifteen

It had been raining heavily all Monday morning, so it came as no surprise to Alfie or any of his classmates when their teacher uttered the two words that most of them simply dreaded hearing: "Wet play."

Or "no football" as Alfie and his friends liked to call it.

Even their attempts to get an indoor game going were quickly scuppered by the presence of the class's teaching assistant, who for once had decided to forego her morning cup of coffee in order to stay in the classroom and keep an eye on the children.

And so it was that during Monday break-time, rather than being outside playing football, most of the Kingsway Colts' players, along with Hayden and Billy, were instead crowded around Danny's desk staring at a piece of paper. On that piece of paper was the latest Middleton District Youth League Under 11s Division 2 league table, which Danny had printed out earlier that morning.

All sets of eyes were immediately drawn to the bottom three positions.

8. Lakeland Spurs	17	5	2	10	29	71	17
9. Kingsway Colts	**17**	**4**	**4**	**9**	**42**	**57**	**16**
10. Heath Hill United	17	4	2	11	32	50	14

With just one game remaining the size of the task facing the Colts was clear for all to see. Even a win may not be enough to get them out of the bottom two. Not if Lakeland Spurs beat Melrose Youth in their final game.

The previous evening, when he'd got round to checking the latest results on his parents' computer, Alfie had initially been pleased to see that Heath Hill had lost once again – 6-0 against Deansview Juniors. However, this pleasure had quickly turned to apprehension as he remembered that the Colts were playing against Deansview in their final match. A match that Deansview themselves needed to win to ensure they finished second.

"Wow," Billy exclaimed, puffing out his cheeks as he examined the league table. "It's so tight."

Everyone nodded silently. There wasn't much else to be said.

After a few seconds of quiet, it was Des who eventually broke the silence. "Oh well, we can only try our best," he stated matter of factly. "If we get relegated, then we get relegated," he added.

Alfie shot Des an angry glance. He was just about to reiterate how important it was that the Colts didn't finish in the bottom two when he remembered that the outcome of the match simply wasn't as important for the rest of his teammates as it was for him.

His dream – his *destiny* – of one day becoming a professional footballer possibly hinged on him staying a Kingsway Colts player. To his knowledge, the same couldn't be said for any of his friends. They could just leave and find new teams, which, of course, is what most of them planned to do if they did get relegated.

For about the thousandth time in the past few weeks, Alfie found himself once again thinking about Madam Zola. He couldn't believe that the fortune teller still hadn't visited him despite all his attempts to find her. He was seriously starting to think that maybe he would never ever see her again, although quite what this would mean for his destiny he had no idea.

Alfie's reverie was broken by Billy repeatedly tapping him on the shoulder. "Guess what, Alf?" Billy began after he'd finally managed to attract his best friend's attention. "Kingsway United's season has already finished, so my Dad has agreed to take me and Hayden to watch your game on Sunday. We can be your cheerleaders," he added with a chuckle.

"I wish you could both play instead of just watch," rued Alfie. "I'd be much more confident about winning then."

Billy smiled regretfully. "Sorry Alf, we're not allowed to I'm afraid. I'd love to play, though. I'm desperate for you guys to stay up. I know how much it would mean to you."

'I'm not sure you do,' thought Alfie, although he didn't say a word. He just nodded and smiled.

"Well I'm going to do everything I can to

make sure we win," Chloe declared. "This will be my last ever game for the Colts and I want to make sure I go out on a high!"

"Me too," Liam echoed. "Not that I'm saying this will definitely be my last game..." he stuttered as Alfie stared accusingly at him. "Not if we win anyway."

"A win still might not be enough, though," Hayden pointed out. "Not if Lakeland beat Melrose..."

"Way to get their hopes up, H," Billy admonished, as Alfie and the others groaned in frustration.

"What?" Hayden asked innocently, as the Kingsway players slowly started to move away from Danny's desk to go and sit back at their own places. "I was only saying."

As he wandered casually back in the direction of his own desk, Alfie was so consumed by thoughts of the coming weekend's game against Deansview Juniors, that he failed to notice that there was someone already sitting in his seat until he was just about to sit down.

"Alright muppet," Jasper called out cheerfully, once Alfie had finally registered the other boy's presence. The larger boy had one of his trademark smirks plastered across his round face. Alfie had seen that smirk often enough to know that this meant Jasper had something in mind. Something undoubtedly unpleasant.

"What do you want Jasper?" Alfie asked, unable to hide the suspicion from his voice.

"I just wanted to wish you and the Kingsway Colts the very best of luck for Sunday," Jasper replied earnestly, before laughing mischievously.

"What do you really want?" Alfie snapped irritably.

"What I said. To wish you luck. I really do want you guys to beat Deansview." Jasper sounded so sincere when he said this that Alfie couldn't help but feel that his long-term nemesis was actually telling the truth.

"Really? Then... thanks Jasper... I guess." Alfie's head was spinning. He couldn't for the life of him work out why Jasper would suddenly want the Colts to win, having been so keen to see the team disband when he'd last spoken to him just a couple of weeks earlier.

The answer was not long in coming.

"Not that it will matter in the slightest

if you do win, of course," Jasper continued, making it clear from the way he said it that he knew something Alfie didn't.

"What do you mean?" Alfie enquired, although he was not all that sure that he really wanted to know the answer.

"One of my Dad's North Malling Town players is having a Birthday party that day," Jasper began. "He's going paintballing all day. I've always fancied going paintballing, haven't you?"

Alfie's whole body bristled. "So what does this have to do with the Colts?" he asked. "Why should I care if one of North Malling Town's players is going paintballing for his birthday?"

"Well I was going to go," Jasper continued, evidently enjoying Alfie's growing annoyance. "But I've decided to go and watch your game instead. Offer you my support. Just like Hayden and Billy. I can be the third cheerleader," he added sarcastically.

Alfie took a deep breath, desperately trying not to give Jasper the angry reaction he was so obviously trying to provoke. "Why?" he asked, trying to keep his voice as even as possible.

"I want to see all your smiling faces for

myself when you hopefully win." Jasper grinned, although it was a far from friendly grin. "I want to see how happy you all are." He paused momentarily. "And then watch all of you – you especially, muppet – crumple to the floor when I have the pleasure of telling you that Lakeland have beaten Melrose, which they certainly will, and your victory means nothing."

"How can you be so sure that Lakeland will beat Melrose?" Alfie scoffed. "Melrose are quite a good team."

"I've heard they are," Jasper agreed. "But five of their players are friends with the North Malling Town player whose Birthday it is." Jasper smiled a wicked smile. Alfie didn't need him to say anything further to know exactly what was coming next. Not that this stopped the larger boy from continuing his story.

"They've all been invited on the paintballing trip, and the great news is that they're all going to go. Unfortunately, well for you guys anyway, this means that Melrose only have seven players available for the match."

Alfie couldn't stop a look of pure horror from spreading across his face. A reaction that only made his nemesis laugh even more cruelly. "The great thing for me," Jasper continued, "is that no matter what happens I can't lose! If you lot get beaten by Deansview, then you'll be relegated. If you win, then Lakeland will beat Melrose and you'll still be relegated. I personally hope you do win – I think that will be a much funnier end to the season. For me anyway."

"Just go away Jasper," Alfie muttered miserably.

"I haven't told you the best news yet," Jasper continued, slowly prising himself up from Alfie's chair. "My Dad's going to watch the Lakeland game and keep me updated with scores. So I'll be able to keep you informed with everything that's happening in the other game. Isn't that kind of me?"

The larger boy didn't wait for a reply. He just strolled off in the direction of his own desk at the back of the classroom, whistling merrily to himself as he went.

Alfie flopped into the chair that had been recently vacated by Jasper, painfully aware that if what he'd just heard was true, then the end of the Kingsway Colts was surely inevitable.

Chapter sixteen

The school week leading up to the Colts'
final match of the season seemed to drag
on forever.

The end-of-Year 6 exams were by now
only a few weeks away and all of that
week's lessons were chock-full of boring
revision and mind-numbingly dull
practice tests. By the middle of the week,
even the class teacher seemed to be a
little bored as, for the umpteenth time
in the past few days, she led her class
through yet another hour of spellings and
grammar preparation.

Yet, while Alfie had tried hard to
concentrate on at least some of what his
teacher was saying, his mind was, as
ever, fixed firmly on football.

Initially he had planned not to share Jasper's news with his teammates. He feared that his friends would give up all hope of avoiding relegation if they discovered that Melrose Youth were unable to field a full team.

Unfortunately, Jasper had other ideas. By the time the bell rang to signal the end of school on Monday, he'd gleefully told each and every Colts player about how his friend's upcoming paintballing day was sure to ruin their chances of survival.

"Do you think he's telling the truth?" Alfie asked Liam as they travelled to the Elite Centre that Wednesday evening.

"Probably," Liam responded. "Why would he lie?"

Alfie pondered Liam's question for a moment. "Maybe he wants us to think that we've got no chance of staying up so that we don't bother trying against Lakeland and definitely lose," he replied after a short pause.

"Yeah... maybe," Liam answered doubtfully.

While it was far from unusual for Alfie to pay less than full attention to lessons at school, it was rather more noticeable when he was too distracted to concentrate fully on football. Yet Jimmy Grimshaw had only been watching Alfie train for less than ten minutes that evening when he realised that something was clearly on the young boy's mind.

Calling him to one side, Jimmy asked Alfie what was up and then listened carefully as the boy told him all about the latest problems facing the Colts.

The elderly coach let out an exasperated sigh as Alfie reached the end of his story. "This is what I hate about competitive football at your age," he rued. "It puts far too much pressure on you. We didn't have websites and things like that when I were a kid, so we never really knew where we were in the league. I suppose our coach might have known, but I honestly can't remember ever being told if we were near the bottom or top. I certainly can't recall ever feeling threatened that we might get relegated to another division... what a horrible feeling that must be for an 11-year-old!"

Jimmy paused and sadly shook his head. "Anyway," he continued, "the best advice I can give you, in fact the only advice, is to forget about the Melrose versus Lakeland game and concentrate only on beating Deansview, which will be a hard enough task in its own right. Nothing you can do can affect the other game's result, so you really do have to try and forget about it and put all your energy into getting the result you need."

While Alfie knew all this already, hearing Jimmy say it made him resolve to ensure that he took no further notice of Jasper's continued barbs and to encourage his teammates to do likewise. The former Kingsway coach even promised Alfie that he would go and watch the Lakeland game, just to make sure that the messages Keith passed on to his son were being relayed accurately. "I'll drive straight over to your game once that one's finished and tell you exactly what's happened, so don't pay any attention to what Jasper says," Jimmy explained, before sending Alfie back into the session.

Eventually, after what seemed like one of the longest weeks in his life, the day of the Deansview Juniors game finally arrived. Alfie had slept surprisingly well during the night and, although he still woke up with plenty of time to spare before Liam and his Dad were due to pick him up, he felt a lot fresher than he had done in the previous two weeks.

Switching on his TV, and quickly muting the volume so as not to wake his parents in case they were still asleep, Alfie kept half an eye on the previous day's football highlights as he gathered together his kit and placed his boots and shin pads into his bag.

He was just about to pluck his so-called lucky teddy bear from the shelf and cram that into his bag as well, when he stopped. For a moment he contemplated whether it was really worth taking the bear with him. He'd spent the last few weeks telling the bear that he wanted to meet up with Madam Zola, yet the Colts' final match of the season was due to kick off in less than two hours and she still hadn't made an appearance.

What's more, if Jasper was telling the truth about Melrose's weakened team, then it seemed his pleas for Kingsway to avoid relegation had also been in vain. Could the bear really be that lucky?

"I'll give you one more chance," Alfie whispered, before taking it from the shelf, asking it one final time for the Colts to win and Lakeland to lose, and then shoving it into his bag.

It was then that he heard the familiar sound of wind chimes chiming.

Chapter seventeen

Alfie's heart skipped a beat as the sound of wind chimes danced merrily in his ears.

"Madam Zola," he exclaimed loudly.

Without further delay, Alfie dashed out of his bedroom and headed in the direction of the noise as fast as his legs would carry him.

Upon reaching the bottom of the stairs, he paused momentarily to try and decipher just where the sound was coming from.

Quickly determining that the much welcomed jingle-jangle of wind chimes was coming from the back garden, Alfie hurried through the kitchen, flung the back door wide open and found himself standing face to face with...

"Megan!" Alfie cried despairingly.

"Morning Alfie," replied his sister cheerfully, oblivious to her sibling's obvious disappointment at seeing her in the garden.

"What are you doing?" he asked, the tone of his voice mixed with equal traces of surprise, sadness and anger.

"Playing with these. They were over there," Megan answered, holding up a wind chime in each hand and using her head to nod in the direction of the garden fence. "I like the noise they make."

"How did they get there?" Alfie asked eagerly, quickly reasoning to himself that maybe Madam Zola had left them hanging on the fence as a clue to signal that she was close by.

His hopes were swiftly dashed.

"Mum put them there. How else do you think they got there silly?" Megan responded, as she continued to make the wind chimes tinkle. "We bought them yesterday while you were at training. She saw them the other week while she was taking you around all those shops and liked them so much that she decided to go back and buy them. She thought you'd like them as well."

"Great," Alfie sighed glumly, before slinking dejectedly back into the house and up the stairs to his bedroom.

By the time Liam's Dad arrived to pick him up an hour or so later, Alfie was still feeling bitterly disappointed about Megan being the source of the jangling wind chimes rather than Madam Zola. He couldn't believe his hopes had fleetingly been raised so high, only to come crashing down in an instant.

However, no sooner had he clambered into the back of Mr Walker's car to take his seat alongside Liam, did his emotions change from those of despondency to nervousness.

It was clear from the look on his teammate's face that Liam was feeling equally apprehensive ahead of the game. Mr Walker did all he could to lift the spirits of his two passengers during the short drive to the Kingsway Recreation Ground, but all his attempts at humour fell on deaf ears as the two boy's stared nervously and silently out of their respective backseat windows.

Arriving at the ground a few moments later, Alfie immediately spotted Luke, Isaac, Will, Billy and Hayden all taking shots at Pranav in one of the park's available goals. Jogging over to join their friends, Alfie and Liam both watched admiringly as Hayden unerringly fired a ball into the top right-hand corner of the net, not giving Pranav any hope of saving it. They were equally impressed when Billy just as spectacularly smashed a ball into the opposite top corner with the very next shot.

"I wish they could both play today," Liam muttered, amplifying the thoughts that Alfie had also been thinking at that very moment.

Within ten minutes the rest of the Colts players, as well as Scott, had joined them by the goal.

The coach quickly set about taking his players through a few warm-up routines and once he'd done this he gathered the children into a huddle around him so he could tell them what the team would be for the match. Not that he really needed to. With Danny still injured, Kingsway's line-up was unchanged from their previous match against Oldhaven a week earlier.

When Ollie's name was read out, Alfie glanced instinctively in the direction of his teammate. It appeared to him that Ollie was paying more attention to flicking mud off the bottom of his boots than he was to what Scott was saying, and Alfie desperately hoped that his friend wasn't going to have one of his distracted days.

"I've heard all the rumours from Danny," Scott explained, once he'd finished confirming the team. "All I can ask from all of you is that you each do your best and put 100 per cent effort into this game. Don't even think about what might or might not be happening between Lakeland and Melrose, and if Jasper does turn up and start trying to wind you all up by telling you the score from that game, just ignore him."

As if on cue, Scott noticed Jasper sauntering cockily in their direction. "Good luck guys. Hope you win," Jasper called out, smiling wickedly.

"He is such an idiot," Chloe mumbled.

"He sure is," Pranav agreed. "I'd love to see his face if we win and Lakeland..."

"What did I just tell you about ignoring him and forgetting about the Lakeland game?" Scott interrupted angrily. "Just concentrate on what you have to do."

Having finished dishing out his instructions for the team, Scott wished his players luck one final time and sent them to line up on the pitch. Within seconds, the referee's whistle sounded to start the game.

What could turn out to be the Colts' last ever match was underway.

Chapter eighteen

Although he was supposed to be playing left midfield, judging by the opening few minutes of the game you wouldn't have known it. Alfie was everywhere.

In the very first minute of the match he'd had to make a lung-busting run back into defence to cover for the daydreaming Ollie as a ball rolled under his foot and kindly into the path of the Deansview centre forward. If it wasn't for a perfectly timed and equally well executed tackle from Alfie then the striker would have undoubtedly had a clear shot at goal.

Within seconds, Alfie was the Colts' furthest player forward, as a long kick from Pranav was flicked on by Liam's head, only for a Deansview defender to get to the ball narrowly before Alfie could reach it.

Although he was trying his hardest not to think about what was going on in the Lakeland game, on a couple of occasions Alfie had sneaked a quick peak in Jasper's direction. Both times he'd been pleased to notice that the larger boy was staring at his phone with a look of annoyance evident on his face.

Alfie was fairly certain that if Lakeland had of scored by now then Jasper would have let the Colts' players know about it. The fact he seemed so angry had Alfie daring to dream that maybe Melrose had even taken the lead. This thought only filled him with more confidence, and the more confident he became, the more impressively he performed.

As half-time approached there could be little doubt that Alfie was having the game of his life. He was winning every tackle he contested, his passes were constantly finding teammates and he was forcing the Deansview defenders to back-track every time he decided to run at them.

He'd even gone close to opening the scoring on two occasions. First with an angled drive from the edge of the penalty area which had missed the intended target by the narrowest of margins, then again when he latched onto a pass from Chloe but, in deciding to work the ball onto his stronger left foot instead of shooting first-time with his weaker right, gave one of the Deansview players enough time to close him down sufficiently to block the shot.

Hayden, Billy and the injured Danny were all loudly roaring their encouragement to the Colts' players from the sideline. They'd even started coming up with a few chants that they were singing heartily – albeit somewhat tunelessly – much to the delight of Alfie and his teammates.

Alfie couldn't stop himself from smiling broadly, and blushing slightly, the first time he heard the spectating trio burst into a rendition of 'there's only one Alfie Jones' after he had made yet another important tackle.

Hearing his friends singing songs about him sent an unexpected surge of pleasure running though his veins. Momentarily, Alfie found himself considering just how elated a professional footballer must feel the first time they hear thousands of supporters singing their name. He would give anything to experience that buzz for himself one day.

However, just two minutes before half-time the noisy spectators were silenced. Isaac hugely over-hit a simple pass back to Des and despite the defender's best attempts to control the ball he succeeded only in deflecting it in the direction of a Deansview attacker. Using the pace on the ball to his own advantage, the Deansview player smashed a first time shot high into the roof of Pranav's goal to put his team ahead. 0-1.

For around half-a-minute the only sound to be heard was the cheering and hollering of the Deansview players as well as their coach, parents and, of course, Jasper – who seemed to be more delighted by the goal than anyone actually connected to Deansview was.

Then, quickly realising that the team needed a lift, almost as one Hayden, Billy and Danny started chanting 'come on you Colts' at the top of their voices.

In spite of the disappointment all of the Kingsway players were feeling at having just conceded the first goal of the game, hearing their friends cheering them on immediately served to raise their beleaguered spirits.

Straight from the kick-off Liam passed the ball to Chloe who set off on a purposeful run aiming for the Deansview penalty area. Some of the opposition players were still half celebrating their goal and, believing that the referee was just about to blow his whistle to bring the first half to a conclusion, weren't concentrating as much as they should have been.

Chloe surged past a couple of sluggish challenges and within seconds had reached the edge of the area.

She was just about to shoot when a Deansview defender finally managed to shrug off his malaise and nip the ball away from Chloe just before her foot could make contact with it. The defender's teammates, however, had evidently still not switched back on and, in spite of the fact the ball landed closer to two Deansview players than it did to him, Alfie managed to reach it first.

Taking one touch to set the ball onto his left foot, Alfie curled an exquisite shot that bounced off the top of the inside far post and nestled satisfyingly into the net. The Colts had levelled immediately. 1-1.

Now it was the turn of the Colts players and supporters to make a noise. A lot of noise. Looking towards the side of the pitch, Alfie was delighted to see that Jasper looked absolutely horrified by this latest turn of events. The former Colts' player quickly glanced down at his phone before grimacing. It was clear that all was not going to plan in the Lakeland match.

Deansview barely had time to restart the game before the referee brought the first half to a close.

Alfie began making his way over to where Scott was standing when he suddenly remembered that he'd left his bottle of energy drink in his bag. "I'll be over in a second," he called out to no one in particular as he pelted off in the direction of his bag to retrieve his drink.

Kneeling on the grass and unzipping the bag, Alfie dipped his left hand in and quickly located the bottle. He was just in the process of pulling it out, however, when his hand brushed against a piece of paper. Having packed the bag himself earlier that morning, Alfie was certain that the only things he'd put in there were his boots, shin-pads, drink and lucky teddy bear. Therefore, he was entirely confused as to what this sheet of paper could be.

Yanking the paper and bottle out of the bag at the same time, Alfie was astonished to see that he was holding a Jane Folies' horoscopes page from one of his sister's magazines.

It looked identical to the one that he'd pulled off his door and thrown into the bin a week earlier, although this page was nowhere near as crumpled as that one had been by the time he'd finished with it, so he knew it couldn't be the exact same one.

Quite why Megan had bothered to get hold of another edition of the same magazine just so she could put that particular page in his bag, Alfie had no clue. He was also a little confused as to when she could have slipped it in there. She'd been outside playing with the wind-chimes the entire time he'd been in his room that morning. 'She must have done it when I went to the toilet,' Alfie reasoned to himself after a moment's thought.

Not that this deduction offered Alfie any hint as to why she was so desperate for him to read this particular horoscope.

Realising that the only way he was going to find out was by actually reading it, Alfie's eyes reluctantly skimmed the

page until he found the Libra star sign. Before he could start reading it, though, he was rudely interrupted. "Reading girl's magazines now are we muppet?" he heard Jasper sneer from over his shoulder.

Feeling majorly embarrassed to have been caught looking at the page, he quickly stuffed it back into his bag. "It's my sister's," he mumbled, without much conviction.

"Of course it is. I believe you," Jasper replied sarcastically. "Your goal was lucky by the way," he added.

"Whatever Jasper," Alfie replied, before standing up, taking a sip of his drink and starting to walk towards the rest of his

148

teammates who were sitting in a circle around Scott.

"The Lakeland score is 0-0 at half-time by the way," Jasper continued, as he followed close behind. "My Dad says that Spurs are all over them, though. Melrose have just got all six of their outfield players behind the ball. Lakeland will definitely score soon."

"You don't know that for a fact," Alfie said, more in hope than expectation.

At that very moment, Jasper's mobile phone beeped. The larger boy took it from his pocket and glanced at the screen. "I do," he grinned. "They've just scored."

Chapter nineteen

By the time the second half kicked off, all nine Kingsway players were aware that Lakeland Spurs had supposedly taken the lead against Melrose Youth.

In truth, it would have been impossible for them not to have known.

From the moment he'd received the text from his Dad, Jasper had been jigging frantically up and down on the spot chanting '1-0 to the Spurs' and 'going down, going down, going down,' as loud as he possibly could.

Scott had urged his players to ignore Jasper's antics, claiming that he might not even be telling them the truth, although the Kingsway coach knew perfectly well that it would be practically impossible for them not to pay any heed to the prancing boy.

Unsurprisingly, the early stages of the second half were dominated by Deansview. The fight seemed to have disappeared completely from every single Kingsway player, all of whom seemed to be resigned to their fate regardless of whether they won their game or not.

Hayden, Billy and Danny were doing their best to try and motivate the team from the sideline, but even their attempts to drown out Jasper's singing were beginning to falter as Deansview continued to carve out, although also thankfully miss, chance after chance.

When an overjoyed Jasper suddenly yelled with pleasure a few moments later, and changed the words to one of his songs to '2-0 to the Spurs', the collective mood of the Colts' players couldn't have sunk any lower.

Alfie himself was almost in tears as he was suddenly struck by the thought that this was almost certain to be the very last game he ever played for the Colts.

It was Chloe who ultimately took it upon herself to try and lift her teammates. "No matter what happens this is my last game for this team," she shouted, as Pranav ran behind his goal to collect the ball, which a Deansview player had just struck a good few yards wide. "I don't know about you lot, but I really want to finish with a win. Who cares whether we get relegated or not. Let's just enjoy playing. Just like Jimmy used to tell us to."

Alfie nodded his approval. If this was really going to be his last game for the Colts, then he also wanted to go out with a victory. "Come on Colts. One last effort," he shouted, although barely any of his teammates seemed to respond to either his or Chloe's words of encouragement.

From the following goal-kick, Pranav passed the ball short to Des, who in turn moved the ball into the midfield area to Isaac. Seeing Liam moving into space up front, Isaac tried to find him with a long, hopeful ball forward. However, not for the first time in the game, he was unable to control the power of his pass and he once again ended up hitting the ball far harder than he had intended to.

Instead of turning and chasing the ball, like he normally would have done, Liam merely shrugged his shoulders and turned away disinterestedly. He would never have admitted it to anyone, but since half-time he'd been starting to imagine how it would feel to be playing for Rickton Rovers next season.

Realising that Liam had no interest in trying to put any pressure on him, the Deansview goalkeeper, who had collected the loose pass, decided to dribble the ball forward himself. With play largely having been confined to the opposite end of the pitch since the start of the second half, the goalie relished the chance of at last finally getting involved in the action.

However, he had been so busy keeping an eye on whether or not Liam was chasing him down, that he'd failed to notice that not all of Kingsway's players were so disinterested in proceedings.

Not until it was too late anyway.

As soon as he'd seen Liam shrug his shoulders, Alfie had taken it upon himself to sprint the entire length of the pitch to apply some pressure on the 'keeper himself.

Catching his opponent completely unaware, Alfie dispossessed him easily and suddenly found the goal at his mercy. Not wanting to make any mistake, he dribbled the ball right into the area before rolling it into the unguarded net as the clearly embarrassed goalkeeper tried in vain to catch him. The Colts were 2-1 up with only 15 minutes left to play.

The goal was met with only muted celebrations, though. While Chloe excitedly leapt on Alfie and offered him her congratulations, the remaining Colts' players either offered him only a half-hearted high-five or muttered 'nice one Alfie' in a far from enthusiastic tone.

Hayden and Billy, however, were dancing wildly with delight on the side of the pitch, while Danny was dancing as much as any boy on crutches actually can.

Jasper had been momentarily silenced by the goal, but he quickly found his voice again. "Doesn't matter anyway, muppet," he goaded, as Alfie moved back into his position to restart the game. "Lakeland are now winning 3-0, so you're still going to go down." Alfie ignored him, determined as he was to concentrate on his own match.

The goal did little to change the flow of the game.

Deansview still continued to apply near constant pressure to the Kingsway goal, desperately searching for the goals that would secure them second place in the table. It was only determined defending from Chloe and Alfie, the only two Colts' outfield players who hadn't given up on the game, and a string of amazing saves from Pranav, who simply hated letting in goals no matter what the situation, that preserved the Colts' lead.

By the time the full-time whistle sounded, Kingsway had somewhat miraculously managed to hold on for the win. Not that any neutral watching the game would have known it. As they shook hands with their opponents, all of the Colts' players looked utterly miserable, certain that the result meant nothing.

As he called his players over to give them their final team talk of the season – and possibly ever – Scott didn't know whether to be happy that they'd won the game, angry at the way most of the players had seemed to give up in the second half, or sad that it looked as though, in spite of their good end to the season, they would still be relegated.

"Get your heads up everyone. We won," he began, somewhat lamely. He really didn't know quite what to say. "Who knows, maybe Jasper was lying. Maybe Melrose have thrashed Lakeland and we've stayed up after all," he said, although he sounded far from convincing.

The children looked at their coach as though he were mad. Surely it was obvious from the way that Jasper was still gleefully dancing around the pitch circle that he was telling the truth.

"We'll know soon enough when Jimmy gets here," he added, making every effort to keep his team's hopes up.

Most of the players didn't even bother waiting around for Jimmy to arrive. They accepted what Jasper had told them and that was that.

Liam and Mr Walker only ended up staying because Alfie pointed out that it would be rude to go before Jimmy arrived as it was him he had promised to see. There was still a part of Alfie – a small part, but a part nonetheless – that believed Jasper could well be fibbing about the Lakeland game.

As the minutes passed by, only Scott, Mr Walker, Danny, Liam and Alfie remained. "He should be here by now," stated Scott, looking at his watch. "Melrose's pitch is only a short distance away. I wonder what's taking him so long?"

The three children and two adults made their way slowly to the car park, figuring that there was no point in making Jimmy walk all the way from his car to the pitch just to tell them something they probably already knew. They had barely got there when Alfie realised that he'd left his bag back by the side of the pitch.

"You'd forget your head if it wasn't screwed on, Alfie," chuckled Mr Walker, who in the months that he'd been ferrying him to and from football had become more than used to Alfie's forgetfulness.

"Back in a minute," the young boy called, as he jogged back in the direction from which he'd just come

When he reached the pitch, however, to his immense frustration, it quickly became apparent that his bag wasn't where he had left it. "Oh no," he moaned loudly. "Someone else must have taken it. I hope it wasn't one of the Melrose players. What else can go wrong today?"

He was just about to return to the car park, when he noticed that there was what looked like a stray bag lying on the ground by one of the goals.

Sprinting over, Alfie breathed a huge sigh of relief as he realised it was indeed his bag. He bent down to pick it up and as he did so heard the roar of a car's engine, swiftly followed by the crunch of tyres on gravel as it pulled into the car park. He immediately recognised the car as belonging to Jimmy and, without even realising that he was doing it, crossed his fingers. "Come on Jimmy," he whispered. "Have some good news for us."

Alfie stood rooted to the spot, unable to move, as he watched Jimmy step out of his car. Yet even from such a long distance away, Alfie could tell instantly from the despairing expression on Jimmy's face that Jasper must have been telling the truth.

Placing both his hands on his head, Alfie groaned as if in pain, as the realisation that he had almost certainly played his last game for the Colts set in.

Would this really mean the end of his dream of one day becoming a professional football player?

Taking a moment to compose himself in order to make sure that he wouldn't break down in tears when he returned to the car park – he didn't want to cry in front of his friends – Alfie was just about to walk back towards the others when he felt someone tap him lightly on the shoulder.

"Hello, Alfie," said a familiar voice.

Chapter twenty

It would be fair to say that Alfie felt absolutely astonished at suddenly finding himself staring up at the smiling face of Madam Zola.

The fortune teller's eyes twinkled with delight as she looked down upon her young friend. It was obvious how happy she was to see him.

Alfie just looked shocked. And a tiny bit angry.

"How are you, Alfie?" she asked merrily. If the old woman noticed the signs of anger present on Alfie's face then she made no sign of showing it. "I can't believe how much you've grown since I last saw you."

"How do you think I feel?" Alfie

responded sulkily, deliberately ignoring the fortune teller's attempt at small talk. "The Colts have just been relegated to division 3, which means most of our players are going to leave, which means that there will be no Colts next season, which means that my dream of becoming a professional footballer won't come true!"

Having been so desperate to see Madam Zola for the past few weeks, he was now infuriated that she'd finally turned up when it was too late.

The fortune teller took a deep breath and was just about to reply, when Alfie continued speaking. "I've been looking all over for you for the last three weeks. You always contact me when I need you, yet this time there's been no sign of you. Where have you been?"

Madam Zola paused for a moment as she considered her response. "I've been busy," she replied eventually.

This time, she could tell immediately from the furious expression on Alfie's face that her straightforward answer had not been considered a satisfactory one. However, before the boy could say anything further, the fortune teller raised her right hand to halt him in his tracks.

"Let's be fair, though, it's not like I

haven't sent you any messages is it?"

"Messages?" Alfie spluttered. "What are you talking about? I haven't received any messages from you!"

"Really?" mused Madam Zola, the confused expression on her face matched the tone of her voice. "What about the fortune cookie?"

At first, Alfie didn't have a clue what the fortune teller was talking about. Then he recalled the fortune cookie that had been included with his family's Chinese takeaway a few weeks earlier. "That was from you?" he asked, sounding truly flabbergasted. "How was I supposed to know that?"

"Did you not look at the piece of paper the fortune was written on?" Madam Zola enquired.

Alfie thought for a moment, and then slowly shook his head. "No. I just threw it back down on the table and forgot about it. How was I supposed to know it had something to do with you?"

Madam Zola smiled. "Well, if you had of looked at it properly then you would have noticed that my initials were printed in the bottom right hand corner." She chuckled to herself. "That's one of the problems with the youth of today. They don't pay attention to anything. Still, I wasn't sure whether you'd pick up on that clue or not. That's why I repeated the message in your sister's magazine."

"Jane Folies' horoscopes page!" Alfie exclaimed, instantly remembering that Megan had pointed out the similarity in the message to him.

The boy scratched his head, wracking his brains to try and make sense of what was going on. "How was I supposed to know that was from you, either?" he asked.

This time the fortune teller frowned. "Oh Alfie," she began, sounding a tad let down. "I am a little disappointed in you. I tried to make it obvious, really I did."

"Make what obvious?" Alfie cried out. He was so confused that he felt as though his head would explode at any minute.

The fortune teller put her left hand into one of her long, green coat's pockets and after a fair amount of rummaging about pulled out a small notebook and a pen. "I chose the name Jane Folies specially," she explained, using the pen to write the woman's name down on a blank page in her notebook. "Don't you see?" she asked, holding the paper out so that Alfie could see it. "Jane Folies is you! Rearrange the

162

letters and you get Alfie Jones. I really thought you would have noticed that," the fortune teller added, scribbling Alfie's name below that of Jane Folies and drawing lines to match the letters.

Alfie's blue eyes opened wide. Seeing and hearing Madam Zola explain this to him made it all seem so obvious.

The fortune teller couldn't stop herself from giggling as she watched the realisation dawn on Alfie's face. Then, just as quickly as she'd started giggling, she just as abruptly stopped.

"Hang on a minute. What do you mean the Colts have been relegated?" she asked, referring back to Alfie's earlier rant.

Alfie was still busy processing Madam Zola's recent revelation, so it took him a few moments to understand her sudden about turn in the conversation. "Erm, Lakeland Spurs beat Melrose Youth this morning, so even though we won today we still got relegated."

A look of pure puzzlement passed across the face of Madam Zola. "It doesn't matter that Lakeland won... wait a minute, did you not get my other message?"

Alfie rolled his eyes. There was no such

thing as a straightforward conversation with Madam Zola. "What other message?"

"The second horoscopes page," she answered. "I'm sure you must have read it."

"You," Alfie proclaimed loudly, pointing an accusing finger at Madam Zola. "It was you that pinned the page to my bedroom door last week and then placed another copy of it in my bag this morning!"

"I'm sure I don't know what you're talking about," answered the fortune teller evasively. "Still," she continued quickly, not giving Alfie the chance to question her any further, "it's clear you haven't read it, am I correct?"

The boy shrugged his shoulders to show that he hadn't.

"Is the page still in your bag?" asked the fortune teller.

Alfie thought for a moment, nodded, and then unzipped his bag, pulled out the page and started to read his star sign aloud.

"It's been a tough and frustrating few weeks for you, but make sure you check all small details and you'll soon see that every cloud has a silver-lining."

He paused, looked up at Madam Zola, and then scratched his head again. "Nope, still don't get it."

Without saying another word, the fortune teller once again plunged her hand into the same pocket from which she'd pulled out the pen and notebook. It emerged a few seconds later holding a ripped piece of paper. "Look at it carefully," she urged, handing it to Alfie.

Displayed on the paper were the bottom four places in the Middleton District Youth League under 11s division 2 table, before the final round of games.

7. Oldhaven Wanderers	17	6	1	10	48	61	19
8. Lakeland Spurs	17	5	2	10	29	71	17
9. Kingsway Colts	**17**	**4**	**4**	**9**	**42**	**57**	**16**
10. Heath Hill United	17	4	2	11	32	50	14

Alfie had to read through the table three times before he spotted what the fortune teller was trying to show him. "We can still finish ahead of Oldhaven if they lost by more than two goals this morning," he blurted out excitedly, his hope that maybe Kingsway could avoid being relegated having been reignited.

Madam Zola smiled warmly and then clapped her hands. "You and your friends were so wrapped up in Lakeland's result that none of you bothered to check the table properly. As I said earlier, young people don't pay attention to anything these days."

"Anyway," said the fortune teller after a short pause, "I should be going." She glanced down at her left wrist. As ever, she wasn't wearing a watch, but things like this didn't seem to matter to Madam Zola. "Wow is that the time! I really must be going. You should be getting back to your friends as well. They'll be wondering where you've got to."

Without so much as saying goodbye, the fortune teller turned briskly and started walking in the opposite direction to the car park.

She'd only gone a few steps, though, when she turned back to face Alfie, who was still trying to digest everything he'd just heard and hadn't even registered that the old lady was leaving.

"By the way, Alfie," she called. "Why did you think that your dream of becoming a footballer wouldn't come true if you were to no longer play for the Colts?"

"Because that's what you told me," Alfie shouted back.

"So I did," replied Madam Zola, as

if suddenly remembering their first meeting. "Well you will actually have to leave the Colts soon in order to fulfil your destiny. But you'll know when the time is right." With that she turned and continued walking off.

Alfie was just about to give chase when he heard his friends calling him from the car park. Torn momentarily between chasing after the fortune teller and returning to his friends, he ultimately decided to do the latter; he'd already been gone far longer that he should have been.

Sprinting back to rejoin his friends, Alfie couldn't wait to tell them that they were not definitely relegated yet, although he wasn't quite sure how he would explain this sudden realisation to them.

As it turned out he didn't have to.

When he got back to the car park, to his complete shock, Liam and Danny were both grinning from ear-to-ear, while Mr Walker, Jimmy and Scott were all happily engrossed in conversation.

"Where have you been Alfie?" Liam asked, his tone sounding strangely excited. The Colts' star striker didn't even allow his friend time to answer the question. "Guess what? We didn't get relegated. Oldhaven did. Jimmy noticed this morning that Lakeland weren't the only team we could have finished above. He looked at the league table before he left the house and saw that we could also have overtaken Oldhaven on goal-difference so he went to watch their game instead of Lakeland's. They lost 5-3 against Southfield."

Alfie's jaw dropped wide open. For half-a-minute he didn't know what to say. Then he remembered the expression on Jimmy's face when he'd stepped out of his car. "Why did Jimmy look so miserable when he got here then?"

"I was trying to fool you," said Jimmy, having noted Alfie's return and wandered over to greet him. "Not a particularly nice thing to do, I know, but you should have seen the look on Liam and Danny's face when I told them the good news."

"Couldn't happen to a nicer bunch," added Scott. "Not after the way that numpty linesperson acted last week."

The boys and Mr Walker all nodded, remembering how the behaviour of the Oldhaven parent had cost the Colts victory a week earlier.

"I'm definitely going to stay next season now," Liam announced. "A promise is a promise after all!"

"And I've already texted everyone the news," chipped in Danny, waving his mobile phone in the air. "Everyone else is going to stay as well. Except for Chloe, obviously."

"I wish I could be there to see the look on Jasper's face when he realises," laughed Liam.

"I can't wait for school tomorrow," agreed Alfie.

"Yep" said Danny. "He's going to be gutted when he finds out that the Colts live to fight another day."

Alfie nodded but kept silent as memories of what Madam Zola had just said came flooding back to him. 'You will actually have to leave the Colts soon in order to fulfil your destiny.'

He was feeling so exuberant at that very moment that he couldn't even begin to imagine ever wanting to leave the Kingsway Colts. Yet if what Madam Zola had told him was right, then his time with the team could be drawing to an end.

And if there was one thing he knew by now, it was that Madam Zola was always right.

Middleton District Youth League
Division 2
Final league table

	P	W	D	L	F	A	Pts
Ashgate Athletic	18	14	3	1	76	15	45
Western Dynamos	18	12	4	2	70	28	40
Deansview Juniors	18	13	0	5	84	31	39
Southfield United	18	9	2	7	55	53	29
Melrose Youth	18	8	3	7	40	51	27
Brook Wanderers	18	5	7	6	35	36	22
Lakeland Spurs	18	6	2	10	32	71	20
Kingsway Colts	**18**	**5**	**4**	**9**	**44**	**58**	**19**
Oldhaven W'drs	18	6	1	11	51	66	19
Heath Hill United	18	4	2	12	35	56	14